I0651721

William A. Hunter

Introduction to Roman law

Fourth Edition

William A. Hunter

Introduction to Roman law
Fourth Edition

ISBN/EAN: 9783742800541

Manufactured in Europe, USA, Canada, Australia, Japa

Cover: Foto ©Andreas Hilbeck / pixelio.de

Manufactured and distributed by brebook publishing software
(www.brebook.com)

William A. Hunter

Introduction to Roman law

INTRODUCTION

TO

ROMAN LAW.

INTRODUCTION

TO

ROMAN LAW

BY

WILLIAM A. HUNTER, M.A., LL.D.,

OF THE MIDDLE TEMPLE, BARRISTER-AT-LAW,

Author of 'Roman Law, in the Order of a Code.'

Fourth Edition

LONDON: WILLIAM MAXWELL & SON.
8 BELL YARD, TEMPLE BAR, W.C.
HODGES, FIGGIS & CO., AND E. PONSONBY, DUBLIN.
THACKER, SPINK & CO., CALCUTTA.
C. F. MAXWELL, MELBOURNE AND SYDNEY.

MDCCCLXXXVII.

EDINBURGH
COLSTON AND COMPANY
PRINTERS

CONTENTS.

———◆———

CHAPTER I.

HISTORY OF ROMAN LAW.

CHAPTER II.

THE LAW OF PERSONS.

CHAPTER III

THE LAW OF PROPERTY.

CHAPTER IV.

THE LAW OF OBLIGATIONS.

CHAPTER V.

THE LAW OF INHERITANCE AND LEGACY.

CHAPTER VI.

THE LAW OF PROCEDURE

PREFACE TO FOURTH EDITION.

THIS book is intended to serve as an introduction to the study of Roman Law, and to give adequate information to those who require a mere elementary knowledge of the subject. On the points of leading importance, a comparison is instituted between the English and Roman Law.

The matter of this book is to a large extent the same as the Institutes of Justinian, but with two exceptions. I have omitted many particulars that were useful to the persons for whom the Institutes were written, but are of little value to a student of modern law. On the other hand —especially in the Law of Property and Contract—the glaring deficiencies of the Institutes are largely supplemented. The object that has been kept in view is to put the student in possession of such information and legal principles as will enable him to acquire a more intelligent comprehension of modern law.

The arrangement follows the order of the Roman Institutional writers. They arranged law in three groups—(1) law concerning persons; (2) law concerning things; and (3) law concerning actions. Practically they subdivided 'things' into—(1) property; (2) obligation; (3) inheritance. 'Inheritance' is discussed in the Institutes after 'property,' and before 'obligation'; but it is more convenient to take it after 'obligation.'

As the present work is intended to serve as a companion to the Institutes of Justinian, the arrangement of Justinian has been, with that exception, substantially followed.

In this Edition a Supplementary Glossary explaining the technical terms and phrases employed in the Institutes will, it is hoped, prove convenient and useful to students.

2 BRICK COURT, TEMPLE,
November 1887.

ROMAN LAW.

―•―

CHAPTER I.

HISTORY OF ROMAN LAW.

THE Roman Law presents two aspects, each Historical value of Roman Law. deserving the attention of the student of Jurisprudence. It furnishes the basis of much of the law of Europe, and has long proved an almost inexhaustible storehouse of legal principles. In the history of legal conceptions, again, it occupies a position of unique value. It forms a connecting link between the institutions of our Aryan forefathers and the complex organisation of modern society. Its ancient records carry us back to the dawn of civil jurisdiction, and as we trace its course for more than a thousand years, there is exhibited a panorama of legal development such as cannot be matched in the history of the laws of any other people.

A

The Priest and the Jurisconsult.

A glance at the earliest authentic legal documents of Rome reveals to us the great advance already made by the Romans as compared with the Hindoos and other ancient peoples. In the laws of Menu or of Moses, law is inextricably mixed up with cosmogony, with religious rites and moral rules. There are not wanting indications of the influence of religious conceptions on Roman Law, but at an early stage the practical Roman mind had drawn a clear line between the office of the priest and of the jurisconsult. The establishment of the Republic emphasized the separation of law from religion. The king was chief pontiff as well as head of the State; but on the abolition of the monarchy the new magistrates were confined to secular affairs, leaving to the College of Pontiffs the undivided care of spiritual matters. To this circumstance may be ascribed in no slight degree the early and rapid progress of the legal institutions of Rome.

Law of Nature.

The Roman genius was essentially practical; to the speculative or theoretical side of Jurisprudence it made no contribution; indeed, such was its poverty in this respect, that it was constrained to import from Greece elementary notions in respect to the foundations of law. The Stoics said the whole duty of man was summed up in one sentence—to act according to nature. By nature they meant a somewhat vague notion of the universe as governed by law, on the moral as well as on the physical side. In looking for such a law, men sought what was common or universal, and not what was peculiar to different communities. It happened that in Rome, when the Stoic philosophy was first introduced, the distinction between the law peculiar to Roman citizens (*jus civile*) and the law applicable to other peoples generally (*jus gentium*) was sharply accentuated. The jurists seized the notion of a law of nature, and proceeded to identify it with the *jus gentium*, so that the two phrases became convertible, with but one exception. The Stoic morality affirmed that slavery could not be attributed to Nature, although it was unquestionably a part of the *jus gentium*. In the passage taken from Ulpian that is found in the Institutes of Justinian, the law of nature is confounded with the instinct of animals; but this blunder only serves to show how slight an understanding of the principles of Stoicism was possessed by Ulpian. The law of nature appears in the legal writings of the Romans as a sort of intellectual garnish, that had no real connection with the Roman Law. It is an idea that explains nothing and illuminates nothing.

The oldest fragments of Roman Law that have *Leges Regiae.* come down to us are ascribed to the period of the

Kings. At Róme, a collection of such laws (*leges regiae*), attributed to *Sextus Papirius*, was known under the name of *jus Papirianum*. Fragments of these laws have been collected from various authors by the diligence of modern inquirers, but we may take the XII Tables as the first solid ground in the history of Roman Law. The agencies by which that Law was developed, by which the scanty rules of the early age of the Republic grew into the *Corpus Juris Civilis* as it was left by Justinian, were three in number—Interpretation by the Jurisconsults, Equity by the Praetor, and Legislation. Before considering these agencies in detail, a brief account of the XII Tables may be given.

XII
Tables.   THE LAWS OF THE XII TABLES.—About the year 450 B.C., a commission is said to have been appointed in Rome to visit Greece, and collect the information necessary to draw up a written body of laws. This suggestion of a foreign extraction for the oldest body of Roman Law, although it seemed in no way incredible to the great jurist Pomponius, can hardly be reconciled with the conclusions drawn by modern inquirers from a wider knowledge of the history of ancient law. But although the XII Tables undoubtedly contain law of indigenous growth, yet they do not give us the oldest law of Rome. Three centuries intervene between the reputed founding of the city and

the XII Tables. During this period, perhaps even earlier, the fundamental institutions of Rome were already undergoing a process of decay. The autonomy of the family, and the absolute authority of its head, were, in the middle of the fifth century before Christ, already shaken. The XII Tables contain provisions enabling a wife or a child to escape from that domestic thraldom upon which society in ancient Rome was based.

One of the most striking features of ancient society is the extreme tenacity with which it adheres to its usages. In some cases the immobility of ancient law may be ascribed to the religious sanction with which it was clothed. The laws are attributed to some divine being, from whose statutes and ordinances it were impiety to depart. But even when laws are attributed to a mere human legislator, there is still a profound dread of change. The attitude of primitive man towards the customs he has been taught to observe, is the counterpart of his timidity in the presence of nature. Man is timid where a being of less intelligence would be cälm, because he perceives countless possibilities of suffering and calamity from the movement of the forces of nature, while yet his experience is too narrow to enable him to tell where evil will arise, and how it may be prevented. Thus, in a backward state of society, any

Ancient Conservatism.

change in the law is both feared and disliked. But in a progressive community, an expansion and growth of law is essential. How that is to be accomplished is the problem of vital interest. In the three agencies that have been enumerated, there may be remarked a progressive openness in *Interpre- tation.* effecting changes in the law. Thus, ostensibly, the jurisconsults do not 'make,' they only 'interpret' law; and yet in numerous cases, by their process of interpretation, they extracted out of the XII Tables a good deal that was never in them. The *Equity.* Praetor, at least in later times, had an acknowledged right to supplement, to develop, and even to change the law, but his power was admitted within circumscribed, although somewhat indefinite, limits. *Legis- lation.* Legislation, the direct and open change of law on account of its unfitness, is the last to reach maturity. Under the Empire, this came to supersede both the others. It is worthy of remark that England affords a parallel case of development. Customary law, as exhibited in decided cases, equity and legislation have appeared in the same order and fulfilled similar functions in England and in Rome.

Jurisccn- sults.　　THE JURISCONSULTS (*Jurisperiti, Jurisprudentes*). —Until the time of Diocletian, the administration of law was not confided to professional lawyers. It was regarded as a public office that each citizen

might be called upon to undertake. The Praetor
was, generally speaking, more of a statesman than
a jurist, a politician on his way to the consulship,
not, as a judge with us, a middle-aged lawyer retir-
ing from active practice to exercise judicial functions. But there grew up in Rome a class of men
who made it their business to know the law and
communicate their information to such as sought
it. Hence a strange result. The men that knew
the law had no direct participation in the administration of justice; the men that administered
justice did not know the law.

Pomponius, in his brief account of the history of *Jus Flavi-*
Roman Law, informs us that the custody of the *anum.*
XII Tables, the exclusive knowledge of the forms
of procedure (*legis actiones*), and the right of inter-
preting the law, belonged to the College of Pontiffs. He goes on to say that this continued for a
century after the publication of the XII Tables,
until Cneius Flavius, a clerk of Appius Claudius,
who had written down the forms of actions, ab-
stracted his master's book and published it. This
publication was known as the *Jus Flavianum.*
Some years later Sextus Aelius wrote a book in
three parts (*jus tripertitum*). It gave an account
of the XII Tables, of the interpretation of the XII
Tables, and of the forms of procedure, and was
called *Jus Aelianum.* Tiberius Coruncanius, who

lived about three centuries before Christ, is said to have been the first to publicly profess to give in-. formation on law. Until, however, about a century before Christ, the task of answering questions of law fell chiefly on aged patricians who had held high office ; but from about that time the existence of a class of professional jurisconsults may be dated.

Responsa Pruden- tium. During the Republic it was entirely voluntary for a magistrate to receive, or for any one to give, advice on law. Nevertheless the ignorance of the Praetor and *judices* naturally led them to welcome such assistance as it was in the power of the juris-consults to offer. But Augustus introduced two important changes ; he gave a higher authority to the opinions of the jurisconsults, while he admitted to the exercise of the profession only those that had first obtained Imperial sanction. Henceforth the *jus respondendi* was confined to the privileged class of authorised jurists. By their opinions those who administered the law must be guided.

Writings of Juris-consults. The authority given to the opinions naturally extended to the writings of the jurisconsults. Hence an extraordinary impetus was given to the production of legal literature ; and to the activity that followed during the first two centuries of the Christian era we owe the rich store of juridical reasoning that constitutes the permanent value of the mature Roman Law.

The system begun by Augustus had one draw- Law of Citation.
back. Jurisconsults might give different opinions,
and how was the person hearing a cause to determine which was right? So marked became the
divisions among jurisconsults, that soon two rival
schools grew up (called respectively Sabinians and
Proculians), giving opposite opinions on a considerable number of points of law. It was thus in the
power of a Praetor or *judex* in many cases to determine his judgment, either for plaintiff or for defendant, according as he chose to follow the Sabinians
or the Proculians. Gaius refers to a partial remedy
introduced by Hadrian. At a later period (A.D.
426) Valentinian enacted a law, commonly called
'The Law of Citation,' providing that the writings
of only five jurists, Papinian, Paul, Gaius, Ulpian,
and Modestinus, should be quoted as authorities.
If a majority of these held one opinion, that was
to bind the judge; if they were equally divided,
the opinion of the illustrious Papinian was to be
adopted.

From the manner in which the jurisconsults Import-
modified the law, it is extremely difficult to specify ance of Jurisconsults.
the changes that ought to be ascribed to them. sults.
Their influence was felt in forms of conveyancing.
Of these the most generally useful was the fictitious suit (*in jure cessio*), which, although resorted
to long before the existence of jurisconsults as a

professional class, was doubtless largely extended
by them. The great bulk of Roman Law, and all
that is most valuable in it, is due to the jurisconsults. A glance at the Collections of Statutes and
Constitutions shows how little relatively was the
amount contributed by direct legislation.

Praetor's
Edict.

EQUITY.—The Praetor exercised a qualified or
limited legislative power. With him all legal
proceedings commenced. By him the questions
at issue between the parties were put into shape.
In a progressive community, where the wants of
the people continually tended to go beyond the
provisions of the law, it was almost inevitable
that the Praetor should exercise on the growth
of Roman Law an influence far more powerful, as
it was more direct and authoritative, than the influence of the jurisconsults. To avoid the evils of
uncertainty, a practice grew up of issuing at the
time of his taking office a Proclamation or Edict
stating the rules by which he would guide himself
in granting or refusing legal remedies. This Proclamation was called *Edictum Perpetuum*, in contrast to temporary or occasional Proclamations,
which were known as *Edicta Repentina*. Naturally
each successive Praetor was content in the main to
follow in the footsteps of his predecessors, and the
portion of their Edict that he transferred to his own
was called *Edictum translatitium* or *tralatitium.*

Until B.C. 66 there was no guarantee, except *Edictum Perpetuum.* constitutional usage, that a Praetor would adhere during his term of office to the rules laid down in his own proclamation; but in that year a statute (*lex Cornelia de Edictis Perpetuis*) was passed, declaring it illegal for a Praetor to depart from his Edict. The growth of this *Edictum Perpetuum* continued vigorously for more than a century after the Empire, although the triumph of the Imperial system involved the destruction of the great elective magistracies of the Republic. Under Hadrian, Salvius Julianus consolidated and arranged the Perpetual Edict; and that work may be taken to mark the end of Praetorian legal reform.

The Praetor stands in Roman Law midway between the jurisconsults and the legislature. His *Jurisdiction of Praetor.* right to alter the law was openly acknowledged, but it was not unlimited. The Praetor was girt round by a firm, although invisible and somewhat elastic, band. He may be viewed as the keeper of the conscience of the Roman people, as the person who was to determine in what cases the strict law was to give way to natural justice (*naturalis aequitas*). But even a wider authority than this was ascribed to him, for he was allowed to entertain general considerations of utility (*publica utilitas*). A single example, however, may suffice to show that the Praetor's edict was confined within real, although

indefinable, limits.   The XII Tables gave the succession to a father's estate to his children under his
potestas; the children released from the *potestas* did
not succeed.   The Praetor, however, did not scruple
to admit emancipated children to succeed to their
fathers ; but it was reserved for later legislation to
provide that a child should succeed to its mother.

Results of
Praetorian
action.

The work of the Praetor may be summed up
under three heads.   It was the Praetor chiefly
that admitted aliens within the pale of Roman
Law.   To him mainly is due the change by which
the Formalism of Roman Law was superseded by
well-conceived rules, giving effect to the real intentions of parties.   Lastly, he took the first and
most active share in transforming the law of intestate succession, by which, for the purpose of
inheritance, the family was regarded as based on
the natural tie of blood instead of the artificial
relation of *potestas.*

LEGISLATION.—To give a full account of this
topic would be to write the constitutional history of
Rome ; suffice it here to mark a few distinctions
that are of importance in looking at the historical
development of Roman Law.

Legis-
lation.

During the Republic, the Popular Assembly was
the fountain of legislation ;[1] during the earlier his-

[1] A statute (*lex*) is what the Roman people (*populus*),

tory of the Empire, the place of the Popular
Assembly was gradually taken by the Senate,
acting as the mouthpiece of the Emperor ; finally,
even this form was dropped, and all enactments
flowed directly from the Emperor.

During the Republic three Assemblies of the Republi-
Roman people existed. The oldest was the can Assemblies.
Comitia Curiata, a patrician body, of which we
have reminiscences in the law of adoption and of
wills. The *Comitia Centuriata*, said to have been
originated by one of the Kings, Servius Tullius,
included the whole Roman people, Plebeians as
well as Patricians, arranged in classes according
to their wealth, but so as to give the preponderat-
ing power to the richest. The *Comitia Tributa*
was based on a local division of the people, the

when asked by a senatorial magistrate—a Consul for instance—ordered.

A decree of the commons (*plebiscitum*) is what the
commons (*plebs*), when asked by a magistrate of the Commons—a Tribune for instance—ordered. The commons
(*plebs*) differ from the people (*populus*), as species does
from kind (genus) ; for the name 'people' means the whole
of the citizens, counting the patricians and senators as
well. But the name 'commons' means the rest of the
citizens without the patricians and senators.

A *Senatus Consultum* (decree of the Senate) is what the
Senate orders and settles. After the Roman people grew
so big that it was hard to bring them together on one spot
in order to ratify a law, it seemed fair that the Senate should
be consulted instead of the people.

vote being taken by wards. In this assembly the
influence of numbers predominated. Livy men-
tions a *lex Valeria Horatia* (B.C. 449) as giving
effect to a compromise between the Patricians
and Plebeians, whereby it was agreed that the
enactments of the *Comitia Tributa* should bind
the whole people. Another law (*lex Publilia*, B.C.
339) seems to have provided that the ordinances
of the Plebeians should be law only with the concurrence of the Senate : the *lex Hortensia*, B.C. 286,
gave full effect to the *plebiscita* without the Senate.
Very often *plebiscita* (such as the *lex Aquilia*) are
called *leges*, a term that in strict propriety ought
to be confined to the enactments of the people
(*populiscita*).

Imperial
legisla-
tion.
    The sovereign power was exercised by the
Emperors in three ways : (1) by direct legislation,
edicta, constitutiones; (2) by judgments in their
capacity as the Supreme Tribunal (*decreta*); and
(3) by *epistolae* or *rescripta*, giving advice on questions of law in answer to inferior judges. This
authority seems to have been conferred by statute
(*lex regia*) at the beginning of each reign. The
law by which Vespasian was invested with supreme
power was discovered in the 14th century; and it
shows that the legal foundation of the Emperor's
power was a statute.

First
Codes.
    The constitutions of the Emperors were col-

lected at different times. The oldest collection is the *Codex Gregorianus et Hermogenianus*, which covers a period of about 200 years, from Hadrian to Constantine. Only a few fragments of it remain. From this period to the reign of Theodosius II. the constitutions are gathered in the *Codex Theodosianus*. This was made by a commission (consisting of sixteen members), appointed A.D. 435, which took three years to the work. It was sent by Theodosius to his son Valentinian III., who accepted it for the Western Empire, and presented it amid acclamation to the Senate. The Theodosian Code has small pretensions to scientific classification. The separate constitutions are collected under titles indicating their subject-matter: these titles are collected in sixteen books. It has come down to us almost complete.

The reign of Justinian marks the culminating period of Roman Law. The production of law had in a great measure ceased before his time, but by a very remarkable series of enactments, Justinian accomplished a marvellous work in cutting away anomalies and giving completeness and symmetry to the body of the law. The chief minister in these reforms was Tribonian, Quaestor of the Palace, who died A.D. 545. Justinian was scarcely seated on the throne when he began the work that has given him such renown. On the 13th

Feb. 528, a commission of ten members was appointed to draw up a Code like the Theodosian Code. In scarcely more than a year (7th April 529) the work was done. This Code, called the *Codex Vetus*, was superseded by a later edition, and has been entirely lost.

Pandects. On the 15th Dec. 530, a commission of sixteen members with Tribonian at their head was appointed for a new task—nothing less than to bring within a moderate compass and arrange in order the vast accumulation of law that had grown up under the hands of Jurisconsults and Praetors. The commission proceeded to deal with the works of 39 jurists, consisting of nearly 2000 books and 3,000,000 verses. In the course of only three years this pile of material was sifted and reduced to about one-twentieth of its original bulk. The scraps or fragments of the jurists were placed under titles, and these were collected in fifty divisions or books. The titles are arranged in Blume's the order of the topics of the *Edictum Perpetuum* discovery. as it was shaped by Salvius Julianus. The arrangement of the fragments under the titles seems to have been mechanical. The commission divided the writings of the jurists into three classes, and assigned each class to a separate sub-committee. The first class, called Sabinian, embraced all the systematic treatises on the *jus civile*; the second,

called Edictal, consisted of the Praetor's Edict,
with commentaries on it ; the third, called Papinian, was formed of the writings of Papinian and
the record of cases. Each sub-committee arranged
its collections independently, and when they came
together to arrange the titles, they took for the
first group that which had the most numerous, and
for the last that which had the least numerous
fragments. Such at least is the conclusion that
has been drawn with much ingenuity by a German
jurist (Blume) from the distribution of the fragments. The finished work was called *Digesta* or
Pandecta, and on the 30th Dec. A.D. 533 it obtained
the force of law.

In the beginning of A.D. 533, a new commission Institutes.
was appointed of law-professors and advocates to
prepare an elementary or preparatory text-book.
The commission adopted the Institutes of Gaius
as a groundwork, and the Institutes of Justinian
are little more than a new edition of Gaius, with
such omissions and additions as were necessitated
by the lapse of more than three centuries. The
Institutes of Gaius were recovered in 1816 by
Niebuhr. Of Gaius himself almost nothing is
known. Even his name is lost, Gaius being
merely a praenomen. Notwithstanding the *lacunae*
that still exist, his work is valuable in reference
to the antiquities of Roman Law.

In the preparation of the Digest, many controverted points turned up, some of which were referred to Justinian for decision. The number of such questions that arose before the Digest was finished was fifty. They were at first collected separately, and called the *Quinquaginta Decisiones.*

After publishing the Pandects and Institutes in A.D. 534, a commission was appointed to revise the old Code, and incorporate the new constitutions and decisions. This revision was completed in the same year, and confirmed on the 16th Nov. 534

Novels. Justinian found his zeal for law reform by no means stifled by these great works, and some of the most important enactments, especially relating to intestate succession, were published afterwards. These subsequent laws are called *Novellæ.*

CHAPTER II.

THE LAW OF PERSONS.

SECT. I.—SLAVES AND FREEDMEN.

THE institution of slavery is ancient and world-wide, but it varied greatly in character and malignity. Among the ancient Hindoos slavery existed, but the number of slaves seems to have been small ; and the indulgence shown by the Hindoo law to the slave contrasts favourably with the harsh theory and practice of the Roman people. But Roman slavery, at its worst, was a humane institution compared with the slavery of the negroes in America, until the civil war of 1860-64. American slavery was a compound of everything that was vile in the laws of various states of antiquity, without any of the redeeming features usually found associated with slavery when it was still a primitive institution. In Rome the difference between master and slave was not embittered by prejudices of race or colour. Slaves were of the same race as their masters—not seldom well educated, and

filling posts of a high and confidential nature.
Slavery was regarded as an accident or misfortune
that might befall any man, not as the natural and
indelible condition of an inferior race.

Legal position of Slave. In the olden times, when Rome consisted of
a small colony of peasant proprietors, few of
whom would be rich enough to possess slaves,
slavery was a domestic institution, and the slave,
in no trivial sense, a member of the family.
Indeed, ancient law makes little difference between sons, wives, and slaves. The children, the
wife, and the slaves of a Roman head of a house
(*paterfamilias*) were equally subject to his unrestricted power, and equally outside the jurisdiction
of the State. If any of them did wrong, not they,
but the head of their house, had to answer for it in
the Courts of the State. In compensation for this
liability, he had the power to surrender the offending person, as a species of slave, in satisfaction to
the complainant (*noxalis deditio*).

Amelio- ration of Slavery. The rise of the imperial power in Rome, while it
depressed the free citizens, was not unfavourable
to the slave. Before the end of the Republic, a
statute (*lex Cornelia*, B.C. 81) was passed, making
it murder for a person other than the owner to
kill a slave, but it was reserved for the Emperor
Claudius to make the crime equally murder when
it was committed by the master. Antoninus Pius,

a devout follower of the Stoics, signalised his reign
by a law providing that masters who ill-used their
slaves should be forced to sell them ; it was even,
he said, for the interest of masters themselves
that relief should not be denied to the victims of
cruelty, or starvation, or unbearable ill-usage. But
although thus protected from ill-treatment, slaves
were not entitled to the privilege of family life, or to
rights of property. A union between a male and
a female slave (*contubernium*) was not a marriage ;
but the offspring, if they afterwards acquired their
freedom, were recognised by the law as related in
blood. Under the title of *peculium*, a slave, with his *Peculium.*
master's permission, might have the enjoyment of
property. Whatever a slave might have as *peculium*, whether the savings from exceptional industry, or gifts as a reward of extraordinary
services, was protected by custom and public
opinion, although not by law. This protection
seems to have sufficed, for the cases were not
rare in which the slave was able to buy his
freedom out of the accumulations of his *peculium.*

Persons were sometimes made slaves as a pun- Captives
in War.
ishment for civil wrongs, but the two chief sources
of the supply of slaves were capture in war, and
birth. According to the barbarous law of war in
ancient times, every prisoner of war was made

a slave.* This was justified on the ground that it was an improvement upon the still more ancient practice of putting all prisoners of war to death.

Slavery by Birth. Again, slavery was hereditary. The children of a female slave were the slaves of her master. It was immaterial whether the father was free or a slave. But though hereditary, slavery was not indelible. Slaves might be manumitted by their masters, and admitted as citizens of Rome.

Formal Manumission. During the Republic, manumission was a formal act (*publica, solemnis*), having the twofold effect of releasing a slave from servitude and enrolling him among the citizens. It required the concurrence of the master and a magistrate, as representing the State. A rare and transient mode was the inscription of the slave's name on the roll of citizens by the Censor at the quinquennial census. But the principal modes were two—one by which the slave was freed in the lifetime of the master, the other whereby freedom was bequeathed as a legacy. The first was called manumission *per*

---

* A Roman captured by the enemy was considered by the Roman Law to be lawfully a slave. But if he effected his escape, and returned to his own country, he was placed, according to the fiction of *postliminium*, as far as possible, in the same position as if he had never been captured. If a *paterfamilias*, he recovered the *potestas* over his family, and the episode of slavery was for the purposes of law obliterated. The doctrine of *postliminium* was also applied to property taken by an enemy, when recovered.

vindictam, a fictitious suit, in which a person claimed that the slave was freeborn. The master admitted the claim, the magistrate made a decree establishing the freedom of the slave, whereupon the master touched the slave with a rod (*vindicta*), and turning him round three times, let him go. Originally testaments were made in the *Comitia* by the authorisation of the people in the usual form of legislation. In this case, the consent of the master and the authority of the people combined to enable a testator to confer freedom and citizen- ship on his slave. This privilege was continued when the testament was not made in the *Comitia*, but became a private act, an instance, of which the history of law records not a few, where an incident attached to an act continues to be attached to it after the reason for its existence has gone.

At first no other mode of manumission was *Latini* allowed. The clearest expression of a master's *Juniani.* *Dedititii.* intention to liberate his slave had no effect unless it was clothed with the proper legal formalities. This led to inconvenient results. If there were a flaw in the manumission, a master might respect his own intention and allow his slave to live in freedom, but his heir, standing on the strict techni- cality of law, might reclaim him back into slavery. At some time not precisely known the Praetor interfered to prevent the scandals that might flow from such a state of the law, and protected the liberated slave in the enjoyment of his personal freedom, although not of his property. In A.D. 19 the *lex Junia Norbana* declared that persons so imperfectly manumitted should enjoy higher rights —the same as *Latini coloniarii.* Persons enjoying freedom under the provisions of the *lex Junia* were henceforth called *Latini Juniani.* They were free, but not citizens, and were subject to various disabilities. If the slave had before manumission been put in chains as a punishment, or otherwise dealt with as a debased person, the *lex Aelia Sentia* (A.D. 4) provided that when manumitted he should be subject to the disabilities of *peregrini dedititii,* and be incapable of becoming a citizen. Before the time of Justinian, however, this portion of the *lex Aelia Sentia* had fallen into disuse, and the name of Latins was rarely heard. Justinian abolished both *Latini Juniani* and *dedititii,* and enacted that whenever a master desired to give freedom to his slave, whether the old forms were observed or not, the slave should become a citizen as well as free.

In the time of Justinian a master was not restricted in the number of slaves he might manumit, unless he released them with the intention and the effect of defrauding his creditors. The other provisions of the *lex Aelia Sentia* requiring a master to be twenty and the slave thirty years of age, unless for special reasons manumission was allowed by a public body, were repealed by him. The *lex Furia Caninia* (A.D. 8), which prohibited a master from manumitting by will more than a certain proportion of his slaves, was also swept away by Justinian.

Manumission did not wholly break the bond Patron's that united the slave to his master. The relation Rights. of master and slave was replaced by the relation between patron (*patronus*) and freedman (*libertus*). The freedman could not sue his patron without first obtaining the consent of the Praetor. The freedman, if he had the means, was bound to support his patron if he fell into poverty. If the freedman had no children of his own, he was bound to leave a portion of his property to his patron ; and if he died without a will and without children, his patron inherited all his goods. Besides, it was usual, as the price of the slave's freedom, that the master should stipulate for a certain amount of work from the freedman. Generally, the freedman worked so many hours in each day. If the patron did not find him food and clothes, he must allow him sufficient time to procure a maintenance for himself. The kind of work was the same as the freedman had been accustomed to as a slave, or any trade he might afterwards learn.

SECT. II.—PARENT AND CHILD.

Powers of Pater-familias.   The powers (*patria potestas*) enjoyed by the head of a household in Rome over his children are scarcely, if we look to the earlier period of the Republic, distinguishable from the rights exercised over a slave. The paterfamilias had, to use the language of the old law, the power of life and death (*jus vitae necisque*). While his father lived, a son could not hold any property, and, however mature his age, could not marry without his father's consent. In early times the father could pawn his children; and a provision of the XII Tables, declaring the paternal power to be forfeited if the father pawned his children thrice, was turned by the ingenuity of the jurisconsults into a means of emancipation. While the Republic lasted, the paternal power was restrained only by public opinion; but under the Empire, it was curbed by the stronger hand of the law. Constantine (A.D. 318) enacted that if a father slew his son, he should suffer the death of a parricide, that is, be tied up in a sack with a viper, a cock, and an ape, and be thrown into water and drowned.

Separate Property of Children.   Considerable progress also was made under the Empire in conferring upon children under the father's power partial rights of property. Thus a son was allowed to keep as his separate property (*peculium castrense*) whatever he acquired as a soldier, and this privilege, under the name of *peculium quasi-castrense*, was extended to many of the higher officials of the 'civil service in respect of their salaries. Finally, Justinian enacted that the father should take only a life interest in respect of every acquisition of a child, except what the child obtained through using his father's property (*peculium profectitium*). The interest of the child in such acquisitions was called *peculium adventitium*.

The Roman family, in the eye of the law, was based on the paternal power. It formed an *imperium in imperio* older than the State. The Roman's house was, in the strictest sense, his castle. The officers of the State did not dare to cross his threshold, and assumed no power to interfere within his doors. The head of the family was its sole representative; he alone had a *locus standi* in the tribunals of the State. If a wrong was done by or to any member of the family, he and not they must answer for it, or demand compensation; if property gained by them were appropriated by another, he, and not they, could reclaim it; if a contract was made with one of them, he alone could sue upon it. The family lived under one roof, had one purse, one altar and one worship. It was this common life and jurisdiction that constituted in the eyes of the early Roman the very essence of the family. A daughter marrying and entering into another household, and becoming subject to a different authority, was no longer regarded (for legal purposes) as a member of the family in which she was born. Her children likewise were strangers to her father's hearth, and not legally of kin to those who continued under his roof. Again, sons released from their father's power by emancipation, ceased to be members of his family. On the other hand, grandchildren descended from sons unemancipated, were in the power of their grandfather, while he lived, and fell on his death under the power of their own father. Even strangers by birth could become members of the family by adoption, and the law originally recog-. nised no difference between them and the offspring of the head of the house.

Acquisition of *potestas.* The paternal power was acquired—(1) by birth, (2) by legitimation, and (3) by adoption. The offspring of a legal marriage were in the power of their father. To this union only citizens could be parties; if either party was not a citizen, their union was recognised as a marriage for many purposes, but not for giving the *patria potestas* to the father. Caracalla extended Roman citizenship to all the subjects of Rome, and accordingly, in the later Roman law, questions as to citizenship did not arise. Constantine introduced *legitimatio per*

subsequens matrimonium, by which in certain cases Legiti-
children born out of wedlock fell under the power mation.
of their father by his subsequent marriage with
their mother. Owing to various causes a species
of morganatic marriage grew up in Rome. The
legal marriage of the Romans was impeded at
different periods by arbitrary restrictions, within
which the impulses of human affection could not
always be confined. A son or daughter could
never marry without their father's consent; and
at one time marriage was forbidden between the
freeborn and freedmen or freedwomen. Such
restrictions did not apply to concubinage, which
was, like marriage, a permanent union of one man
with one woman, although considered not so
honourable, especially on the part of the woman.
It was to children born of such a union, and to
them only, that legitimation applied. By the subsequent marriage of their parents, they fell under
the power of their father.

Until Justinian altered the law, adoption was a Adoption.
mode of acquiring *potestas.* He enacted that it
should continue to have that effect only when a
father adopted a child, or a grandfather adopted
a grandchild; and that in all other cases adoption
should not confer the *potestas,* but give the adopted
child merely a right of succession in case the
adopter died without leaving a will. In the

time of Justinian adoption was nearly as much
out of harmony with the requirements of social
life as it is now. But adoption occupies an interesting place in the history of law. It formed an
intermediate stage of progress between the ancient
law, which recognised nothing but intestate succession and the later law, which possessed in the Will,
a more perfect instrument to settle the devolution
of an inheritance. The oldest form of adoption
(*arrogatio*) was effected by the legislative authority
of the *Comitia.* Only persons who were not under
any one's power (*sui juris*) could be adopted in
this way. By taking advantage of the provision
of the XII Tables, declaring a forfeiture of the
potestas, if the father thrice pawned a son, and by
calling in aid a fictitious suit (*cessio in jure*), persons were enabled to adopt those who were *alieni
juris*, that is, under some one's power. In later
times, arrogation was effected by rescript of the
Emperor, and simple adoption by a declaration in
the presence of a magistrate.

Emanci-
pation.   The paternal power was dissolved by the death
of the paterfamilias, or by any thing that deprived
either father or child of the status of a Roman
citizen. It could also be terminated at the will of
the father, by a declaration before a magistrate.
This simple act replaced the elaborate proceedings
that anciently were required for the emancipation

of a child. Here it may be sufficient to observe, without going into somewhat intricate detail, that the last stage in the process of emancipating a son was precisely the same as occurred in the manumission of a slave. From this a singular consequence followed. The duties and rights of an emancipated son were identical, except in one point, with those of a freedman. The father could not exact a promise of work from his son ; the son owed his father reverence, said the Praetor, not menial work. The emancipated son could not sue his father, except in a fit case, and with the leave of the Praetor; he was bound to maintain an indigent father. The father, in like manner, was bound to support an indigent son. The relation of a father to an emancipated son governed the wider relation of parent and child. The obligations between a parent and child, where the *potestas* did not exist, were the same as the obligations between a father and his emancipated child.*

---

* *Capitis deminutio.* — *Caput* included three elements, freedom, citizenship, and family rights. The loss of freedom, as when a person was captured by an enemy, was *maxima deminutio capitis*. The loss of citizenship, as by the punishment of deportation to an island, was *media* or *minor deminutio capitis*. A change of family, by adoption, or arrogation, or emancipation, was a *minima deminutio capitis*.

SECT. 3.—HUSBAND AND WIFE.

Wives *in manu.*   While the powers of the Roman father over his children appeared even to the Romans themselves as singular, the relation that subsisted between husband and wife during the greater portion of the Republic and the whole of the Empire, presents in a different way an equally conspicuous contrast with the laws generally prevailing in Christendom. There was, indeed, a stage in the history of Rome when the position of a wife was almost identical with that of a slave or child under the paternal power. A wife *in manu viri* could enjoy no rights of property, and she was described, not inaccurately, from a technical point of view, as the daughter of her husband. The marital power (*manus*) appears under two aspects. On the one hand it had a reverential and religious aspect. It was created by a religious ceremony (*confarreatio*), and only the offspring of such a union were eligible as candidates for the higher priestly offices. Here the subjection and dependence of the wife were hallowed by religious associations. On the other hand, the Roman *manus* shows a baser, and perhaps more intelligible, origin. The woman was sold to the husband, and conveyed by the same forms as if she were a slave. So strictly was the wife assimilated to property, that if she were delivered to the husband without the proper forms of conveyance, she did not fall under his *manus* until the usual period of prescription had passed. It was by taking advantage of this circumstance that the Romans were able to get rid of the *manus* almost entirely. A title by prescription could not be acquired unless the possession were continuous; and accordingly, if a wife absented herself, and returned to her father's house before the year of prescription had run out, the prescription was broken. So early as the XII Tables, this mode of avoiding the *manus* had acquired the constancy of a custom. They contain a provision fixing three nights as the extent of absence that prevented the husband acquiring *manus* by prescription. The *manus* had almost disappeared before the end of the Republic, and under the first emperors was looked upon as a mere antiquarian curiosity.

The mode of escape from the *manus* was one that did not merely mitigate or alleviate the harshness of female subjection, but one that wholly swept it away. A wife was either in the *manus* or out of it. If she was *in manu*, the despotic powers of the husband knew scarcely any limit; if she was not, the wife remained in the power of her father—in law a member of her father's family—and wholly free from

Status of Wife.

C

the power of the husband. Thus the only legal consequence of a marriage was that the offspring were under their father's power, and enjoyed rights of inheritance ; between husband and wife there was no bond of legal duty. The wife could not compel her husband to maintain her ; the husband had no rights to the wife's property, except such as were given him by prenuptial contract.

Divorce. If the husband or the wife were not satisfied, the remedy was divorce. It was not necessary to obtain the authority of any tribunal for the dissolution of the marriage; by a simple formal intimation either party could at once terminate the union. While the Roman jurists gloried in the ancient maxim of their law that marriage should be a free union, the ecclesiastics, who acquired an influence over legislation by the conversion of the Emperor Constantine, set themselves with inflexible resolution to uproot the ancient freedom. Upon the principle of divorce by mutual consent they were unable to encroach, but they succeeded in obtaining enactments from successive emperors confining the right of repudiation by one party alone to cases where the other had been proved guilty of gross misconduct.

Custody of Children. If neither party was in fault, the general rule seems to have been that the father took the custody of the boys, and the mother of the girls ; if the divorce was owing to the fault of the father, the wife was entitled to the custody of the children, and the father was obliged to maintain them ; if the mother was in the wrong, the father obtained the charge of the children.

The peculiar conflict that emerges in the Roman *Dos.* Law between the rights of the father and of the husband is connected with an institution that has exercised a vast social and economical influence. Marriage gave the husband no claim of any sort upon the wife's property. But he was under no obligation to maintain her. The Roman point of view seems to have been that it was the duty of a father to maintain his daughter, notwithstanding that she was married. But as it would have been practically impossible to perform this duty day by day and week by week, when the daughter lived under her husband's roof, the father once for all compounded with the husband by giving him a sum down. This sum was called *dos*) By a statute (*lex Julia*), which dates from the transition period between the Republic and the Empire, every father was compelled, on the marriage of his daughter, to give her a *dos* if he had the means. The husband. enjoyed the use of the property during the marriage, but on its dissolution, whether by death or divorce, the property reverted to the wife's father. If the *dos* was given by a paternal ancestor, it was said to be

profectitia; if it was given by the wife herself, or by
any other person than a male ascendant, it was called
adventitia. When a person so gave a *dos,* it was
understood to be a present to the wife after the
dissolution of the marriage, unless it was specially
agreed that it should revert to the donor, in which
case it was called *receptitia.* There are distinct
signs that in the beginning the husband's rights
over the *dos* were more extensive than they afterwards became, and the tendency of the later law
was to restrict the husband rigorously to the in-
come of the property, and not to give him power
of disposing of the capital. Thus he could not
sell or mortgage his wife's lands even with her
consent.

Donatio
propter
Nupti. s. The *dos* was usually the subject of a prenuptial
contract ; but it might be commenced or increased
after the marriage. During the later empire, a
settlement might be made on the wife by the
husband of a nature corresponding to the *dos,*
and was called *donatio propter nuptias.* The predecessor of Justinian allowed such gifts to be
increased after marriage, thus breaking in upon
a rule very jealously guarded by the older law,
that no gifts were binding between husband
and wife. A gift by a husband to a wife, or by
a wife to a husband, could be revoked by the
donor at any time during life. The provisions

of the Roman Law thus furnish a singular con- English Marriage Settlement
trast to the leading characteristics of an English
marriage settlement. A settlement usually gives
an interest in the property to the offspring of the
marriage ; but in Rome the children had no
interest in the *dos*. By the clause in restraint of
alienation, a wife is prevented from giving away
the capital of her property to the husband, but it
is only by depriving her of the power of alienation
in regard to everybody else : while the English
law makes no provision to protect feeble husbands
from avaricious or extravagant wives.

Sect. IV.—Tutors and Curators.

The office of tutor in the Roman Law ap- Functions of Tutor.
proaches nearly to that of a trustee. The tutor
was appointed to act on behalf of children under
the age of puberty, but his duties differed con-
siderably from the duties of an English guardian
of children. The tutor did not himself undertake
the custody and education of the pupil entrusted
to his care. If the will appointing the tutor did
not name any person for that duty, the mother of
the children was entitled to the custody of them
so long as she remained unmarried. It was only
under special circumstances that the tutor could
determine the sum to be allowed to his pupil for
maintenance ; as a general rule, unless it were

fixed by the will, the sanction of the Praetor
must be obtained. The duty of the tutor was to
manage the property of the pupil, and authorise
him to bind himself by contract (*et negotia gerunt
et auctoritatem interponunt*, Ulp. Frag. 12, 25).
In dealing with the property of the pupil, the
tutor was subject to rules such as now govern
trustees. He was bound to make good all loss
sustained by his neglect or wilful wrong ; he was
bound to take such care and so manage the property as a good head of a family would manage
his household affairs ; he could charge nothing
for his services, and he was not allowed to obtain
any advantages for himself, but must exercise all
his power for the sole benefit of the *pupillus.*

Disabili-
ties of
Pupil.
Although a pupil had no property, he nevertheless had need of a tutor. A child could not bind
himself by contract, and there were some legal
transactions, as acquiring an inheritance, which
although in a particular case they might be
wholly beneficial to him, yet required the authority of a tutor. The simplest course would have
been to hold that no person under the age of
puberty could enter into any legal transaction ;
and to make the tutor a statutory agent, whose
acts within the scope of his authority should bind
the pupil's estate. That was not the theory of the
Roman Law. The theory was as far as possible

to make the child the actual contracting party, but not to bind him unless the tutor was present to give his consent (*auctoritas*). Until the child passed his seventh year, and entered on his eighth (*pubertati proximus*), he was not considered capable of so binding himself, even with his tutor's authority ; accordingly, if any action were brought by _ or against the *pupillus* up to that age, the tutor acted for him in his own name ; but if he were above seven, the suit went on in the name of the pupil, the tutor merely giving his sanction. The rule prohibiting a tutor from getting any advantages from his trust, equally prevented the validity of any contract by which he authorised an obligation beneficial to himself (*regula est juris civilis, in rem suam auctorem tutorem fieri non posse*).

The general rule determining the incapacity of a child was that he might better his condition, even without the authority of the tutor, but he could not make it worse, unless he had his authority. In such contracts as create obligations for both contracting parties, as sale or letting to hire, if the tutor did not give his authority, those that contracted with the pupil are themselves bound, but he is not in turn bound to them. This rule was subject, however, to equitable restrictions in favour of the contracting party. A pupil could throw up a purchase, but he could not keep what he had

Contracts of Pupil.

bought and refuse payment, or demand back what
he had sold without giving up the price.

Appoint-
ment of
Tutors. Tutors were appointed by will or upon intestacy ;
failing both, by the magistrate.   At first testa-
mentary tutors could be nominated only by a
paterfamilias to those under his power; but the
Praetor confirmed, either as of course, or upon inquiry as to the fitness of the tutor, the appointment
by a father who had not the paternal power, or by a
mother.   Failing testamentary tutors, the kin were
obliged to undertake the duty to the children
(*legitimi tutores*).   In the ancient law, the agnatic
kin thus succeeded ; but Justinian left it to the
next of kin, whether agnatic or cognatic.   In
default of kin, the *Lex Atilia* (B.C. 197) gave the
urban Praetor and a majority of the tribunes of the
Commons the power of appointing tutors, and the
Lex Julia et Titia (B.C. 31) gave a similar power
to Presidents of Provinces.   Appointments under
those statutes fell into disuse, and in the time of Jus-
tinan the Prefect of the city of Rome, or the Praetor,
and, in the Provinces, the Presidents, after inquiry,
or the magistrates, by order of the Presidents, appointed tutors (*tutores dativi*).

Exemp-
tions from
Tutela. The office of tutor was obligatory on those who
were duly nominated. But the inconvenience arising
from that rule led to the establishment of numerous exceptions (*excusationes tutorum*), which are

minutely described by Justinian, but are of little interest at the present day. Before entering upon the discharge of his duties, the tutor, if *legitimus*, was required to give security: testamentary tutors were exempt from giving security; in the case of 'those appointed by the magistrates, after inquiry, none was required; but those appointed by the inferior magistrates must give security.

The tutela ended with puberty, which was fixed End of at twelve for girls and fourteen for boys. But even Tutela. before that, tutors could be removed by the Court for misconduct or unfitness.

The old law, which made puberty the age of Minors. legal majority, was obviously defective. Accord- Curators ingly, while in strictness every legal act by a person above the age of puberty was valid, a practice grew up of rescinding (*restitutio in integrum*) any bargains or conveyances made by persons above puberty, but under twenty-five, if the contract was an imprudent one for the minor. This cure might have been worse than the disease, had it not been that a minor could obtain the appointment of a curator, whose consent to the transaction, given in like manner with the consent of a tutor, made it unimpeachable. But except for that purpose it was not essential that curators should be appointed to minors. Curators could be appointed also to lunatics, the deaf, the dumb, incurables, and spendthrifts. Spendthrifts (*prodigi*) were those who, in consequence of wasting their property, were prohibited by the Praetor from the management of it. The duties and mode of appointment of curators are almost exactly the same as in the case of tutors.

CHAPTER III.

THE LAW OF PROPERTY.

Sect. I.—Ownership.

THERE is no point on which the theoretical speculations of writers like Blackstone have been more completely falsified than the question of the origin of property. The suggestion that ownership arose when men began to respect the rights of the first occupier of what was previously appropriated by no one, is curiously the reverse of the truth. Conclusive evidence has been brought forward to show that when ownership is first recognised, it is not ownership by individuals, but ownership by groups—the family, the village or commune, the tribe or clan. Individual property arose from the breaking up of such groups, and the distribution of the rights of the whole among the members. In some cases this process was hastened by wars. There are distinct traces that individual property was pre-eminently that which the warrior had seized as the spoil of victory; among the Romans, for example, the spear was the highest symbol of property.

Ancient Communism. But the student of Roman Law will learn nothing of this widespread primeval communism from the works of the Roman jurists. From the earliest times of which we have a record, the institution of private property was completely developed in Rome, and hence the singular influence it has exerted on the destinies of European nations.

Defects of Old Law. The law of property in Rome was in the beginning marked with two characteristics which became increasingly inconvenient as her empire extended. The modes of conveying property were ceremonial and cumbrous, and only citizens of Rome could be owners. Few articles of any importance in ancient times could be conveyed without mancipation, a ceremony thus described by Gaius :—

Mancipation. ✓ '*Mancipatio* is a fictitious sale ; and the right is peculiar to Roman citizens. The process is this :—There are summoned as witnesses not less than five Roman citizens above the age of puberty, and another besides, of the same condition, to hold a balance of bronze, who is called the *libripens.* He who receives the object *in mancipio,* holding a piece of bronze (*aes*), speaks thus :—"I say this slave is mine *ex jure Quiritium,* and he has been bought by me with this piece of bronze and balance of bronze." Then with the piece of bronze he strikes the balance, and gives the piece of bronze, as if the price to be paid, to him from whom he receives the object *in mancipio.'*—(G. 1, 119.)

The objects that required mancipation included *Res man-*
not merely land and houses, but slaves and beasts *cipi.*
of draught and burden.

When a *res mancipi* was delivered to a buyer Quiritarian
without *mancipatio*, the ownership still remained and Boni-
with the seller. But according to the old law, Ownership.
this evil was not without a remedy. For it was
held that where a man possessed a thing in good
faith for two years in the case of land or houses,
and for one year in the case of other things, he
became owner by prescription (*usucapio*). Lapse
of time thus served to cure defective titles in
all cases where a mere informality stood between a man and the ownership to which he was
entitled. One difficulty alone remained. If the
possessor by accident lost possession of the thing
before the time of *usucapio* had run out, he could
not sue as owner, because his title was not yet
complete. This defect was removed by a Praetor
of the name of Publicius (who may have been the
Quintus Publicius said to have been Praetor
in B.C. 66 by Cicero), who gave an action (hence
called *actio Publiciana*) to a possessor under those
circumstances. Henceforth the position of a
possessor of a *res mancipi* delivered without
mancipation was for all practical purposes as
good as ownership. Even before his title was per-
fected by *usucapio*, he was secured in the practical

enjoyment of the ownership. This form of ownership is called by Theophilus—the first commentator on the Institutes of Justinian—Bonitarian ownership, to distinguish it from Quiritarian ownership (*dominium ex jure Quiritium*). When at length *mancipatio* fell into disuse, before the time of Justinian, the distinction vanished, and all kinds of property, moveable or immoveable, were transferred by simple delivery.

Possession.
Aliens.

The second great defect of the old Roman Law was more difficult to remove. At first no stranger had any *locus standi* before a Roman tribunal : he could not hold property, or make a contract, or even sue for a wrong. This exclusive system was inconsistent with the world-wide dominion Rome was destined to achieve; and in nothing is the legal genius of the Roman people more conspicuous than the skill with which they made the narrow principles of the ancient law yield to the necessities of the law of progress. In the case of ownership the process by which aliens were secured in the enjoyment of rights of property was simple but effective. The Praetor could not give to aliens the *dominium ex jure Quiritium*, but he could use his power to secure them in the actual enjoyment of the objects of property. He could punish anyone who trespassed on the alien's land, or who attempted to eject him from his holding. It was part of the policy of the Praetor's innovation scrupulously to respect names, while altering things; and thus he professed not to give ownership, but only *possessio*. To protect this possession, the Praetor granted special actions, called Interdicts. Possession was thus ownership in substance, in everything but in name. Such is the simple explanation of a subject that has introduced more confusion into jurisprudence, and been the occasion of calling into the world more cartloads of learned legal and metaphysical treatises, than all the other topics of Roman Law put together.

The disrepute into which the ceremony of *mancipatio* fell, and the anxiety to make simple delivery suffice for the conveyance of all kinds of property, was strengthened remarkably by the Praetorian law of Possession. Delivery was the natural mode of transferring possession. Delivery was thus the authorised mode of conveying the species of property recognised by the Praetor; and even Roman citizens were glad to rest content with this conveyance and the rights it conferred. To accidents such as these the Romans owed the fact that the only mode of transferring Ownership was the delivery of possession, a mode which although not inappropriate in the case of moveables, became inconvenient when it was sought to convey lands

Transfer by Delivery.

at a distance (*Traditionibus et usucapionibus dominia rerum non nudis pactis transferuntur*, C. 2, 3,

20). Delivery took place, of course, by actual transfer of physical possession ; but without that, it might be effected by placing the thing within view of the person to whom it was meant to be transferred, and declaring that he was free to take possession (*longa manu*). Delivery of the keys of a house or warehouse was sufficient to transfer the property either in the house itself or its contents. Putting marks, as upon logs of wood, was another way of effecting legal delivery, where it would have been difficult to have an actual dealing with the physical possession. To deliver a thing at a man's house was considered the same thing as delivery to himself. If the person to whom it was sought to transfer the ownership was already in actual possession, the ownership could be transferred by a mere expression of a wish to that effect by the owner. That was called *brevi manu*. Mere physical delivery, it must be borne in mind, did not alone transfer the ownership ; it did so only if the owner made the transfer with that intent. In the case of sale, something more was required. The buyer did not become owner by delivery even, unless the price were paid or the vendor gave the

buyer credit.

The English law of sale offers a conspicuous

contrast upon this point to the Roman Law. Delivery is not necessary in the English law to transfer the ownership of the thing sold. Whether upon a contract of sale the goods pass to the buyer with or without delivery, is a question solely of the intention of the parties. If that intention is expressed, there is an end of the controversy. Generally speaking, however, no intention is expressed, and then certain presumptions of law come in. If specific ascertained goods are sold unconditionally, the property immediately vests in the buyer, unless it can be shown that such was not the intention of the parties. If the goods are not ascertained, no property passes until they are identified or 'appropriated' in terms of the contract. If specific goods are sold subject to a condition, the general rule is that the property does not pass until the condition is fulfilled.

If the person who delivered a thing was really the owner, then the delivery at once operated to give the ownership to the transferee. If he was not owner, the delivery had not that effect, because no one can transfer to another greater rights than he has himself. (*Nemo plus juris ad alium transferre potest quam ipse haberet.*) The defect was curable by prescription. If a person at the time when any thing was delivered to him did not know any defect in the title of the transferror, and

D

believed that he obtained the ownership, he was said to be a *bona fide possessor*, and was in a condition to become owner if he continued in possession for the time required by law. Justinian fixed the period at three years for moveables; ten years for immoveables, if both the possessor and the person claiming adversely lived in the same province during the whole time; and twenty years if during the same period they lived in different provinces. But the possession must be uninterrupted. This did not mean that the articles should not change hands. Each person who took the thing in ignorance of any defect in the title could add to his own time of possession (*accessio possessionis*) the times of possession of all his predecessors who were in the same blissful ignorance.

Stolen Goods. In the case of moveables, however, it was but rare that a possessor got any benefit from his innocence. If the thing had been stolen, it could not be acquired by prescription by any length of time. The taint thus attaching to stolen goods could not be removed until they got back to the possession of the owner. A similar taint attached to land or houses from which the owners had been driven by violence. Even a *bona fide* possessor in that case did not acquire by prescription.

Positive and Negative Prescription. The rules just stated illustrate the nature of positive prescription as distinct from statutes of limitation or negative prescription. In the case of positive prescription, the conditions of ownership depend upon the mental state of the possessor, limited by the stringent rule that stolen goods and lands seized by force are incapable of being so acquired. The dominating purpose of the old *usucapio* was in fact merely to cure informalities in the mode of acquisition. Negative prescription means that the true owner is debarred of his legal remedy if he neglects to seek the aid of the tribunals for a given time. Here the law contemplates distinctly divesting the true owner of his rights, but without giving the possessor any positive title. It was unimportant what was the state of mind of the possessor, or whether there was any taint in the article. At first, Roman Law had no statute of limitation, but in the time of Justinian the period for actions generally was thirty years.

Another important mode of acquiring owner- *Occupatio* ship was *occupatio*, or the taking possession of a thing belonging to nobody (*res nullius*), but capable, neverthless, of being held in ownership. In the eyes of the Romans, all untamed living creatures, whether their habitat is the air, the land, or the sea, were *res nullius*, and became the property of the person by whom they were captured. Rome Game. had no game laws. A man might be forbidden to Laws.

go upon another's land to hunt or snare birds ; but if he went and actually caught any bird or beast, they became his property. A bird or beast that was wounded belonged to him that actually took it, and not to him that struck the blow. If a wild creature after being caught escaped either out of sight or practically out of reach, it was again considered *res nullius,* and open to the first captor.

Tame Animals.
Domesticated and tamed animals were not *res nullius,* and any appropriation of them without the will of their owner was theft.

Pigeons
Pigeons and peacocks and birds might go beyond the reach of their owner, but yet return. So long as they did not lose the habit of returning, they were considered as domes-

Bees.
ticated animals. When bees hived, the young swarm belonged to the owner of the bees so long as he kept them in view and could follow them up ; otherwise they became the property of the first

Precious Stones.
person that hived them. Precious stones found in a state of nature also became the property of the

Treasure-trove.
first taker. Treasure-trove, that is treasure left in the earth by persons unknown for a long time, belonged half to the finder and half to the owner

Enemy's Property.
of the ground. Lastly, the property of an enemy was *res nullius.* To this barbarous doctrine the Roman Law recognised no limitation. Lands, houses, moveables, wife and children—the enemy himself if alive—all became the spoil of the captor.

The last mode of acquisition is Ac<u>cess</u>ion. Acces- *Accession* sion is of four kinds :—(1) of land to land ; (2) of moveables to land ; (3) of moveables to move- ables; and (4) the addition of labour to moveables. The first case of accession of land to land arose from the action of streams and rivers in altering the distribution of land. In its higher reaches a river impetuously denudes patches of land, which, as its velocity diminishes, it gradually deposits. The slow increase of land near the mouth of a river, so gradual as to be at each moment impercep- tible, was called *alluvio*, and the increase belonged *Alluvio.* to the owner of the lands enriched by the accre- tion. If the deposit takes place in the bed of the river, gradually an island is formed. The owner- ship of such an island was determined by its posi- *Islands* tion in the stream. If it lay wholly to one side of *formed in Rivers.* a line drawn longitudinally through the middle of the stream, it belonged to the owner of the land on that side of the river ; or it was divided among them if there were more than one such owner according to the extent of their lands, measured by straight lines drawn across the river from their respective boundaries. If the island lay in mid- stream, or partly on one side, and partly on the other, of a line drawn down the middle of the stream, then it belonged to the owners on both banks, and that line became the boundary between

them. If an island were formed by a river chang-
ing its course, forking into two branches and unit-
ing lower down, the ownership of the land so
surrounded was not changed. If a river perma-
Old Beds nently alters its course, leaving its old bed dry,
of Rivers. that bed belongs to the landowners on both banks
of the river, divided in the way already stated
when an island arises in mid-stream.

Fixtures.   Moveables accede to land when one man sows,
plants, or builds on another's land. The maxim
of the Roman Law was that every thing fixed
into the land upon its surface became the property
of the owner of the soil. The owner of the principal was the owner of the accessory. In its
primary aspect, the notion of a principal and accessory is arbitrary, although not illogical. Dress
exists for men, not men for dress ; dress is an
accessory, because it exists for the sake of men.
The ground upon which a pillar rests is the principal, because it can exist without the pillar, but
the pillar cannot exist without the ground. This
arbitrary idea was used to determine a difficult
technical question. When land was built upon,
and the land did not belong to the person who
built, a conflicting claim of ownership arose. It
would have been impossible to consider the landowner and the house-owner jointly owners, for who
was to determine their respective shares ? Hence

in all cases where the materials of different persons got so intermixed that it was inexpedient to separate them, the question of ownership was determined by the rule that the owner of the principal should have the accessory. At first the Roman Law was content to let the question rest there : whatever was built on the land belonged to the owner of the land ; but a question of equity remained behind. Suppose the owner of the land built Compensation. with material belonging to another. Then the XII Tables provided that the landowner should, in that case, pay double the worth of the material to the owner of the material. Suppose the owner of the material built on land not belonging to him. He either knew that, or he did not. If he knew it, he acted with his eyes open, and lost his property ; but if he thought he was building on his own land, the Praetor ultimately protected him from ejection, unless the owner offered compensation. If, however, he accidentally lost possession, and the owner recovered the land without the necessity of a lawsuit, he had no remedy. To this rule the Roman Law admitted one just and politic exception. A tenant of a house could remove the fixtures that he had placed for his use, provided he did no damage to the house. Unexhausted Improvements. A tenant of land was entitled to compensation for unexhausted improvements, except such as he had specially agreed to execute in consideration of a lower rent. The amount was fixed with regard to the increased value of the land.

The idea of accession was employed in the case of addition of moveables to moveables ; such, for **Books** example, as writing a book, or putting gold letters **Pictures.** on paper ; but in the case of pictures, it was thought too strong to say that the ownership of the canvas or wood should determine the ownership of the painting. In this case the logical idea succumbed to the test of value. The rules as to compensation came in as in the former case to redress the balance of unfairness.

Manu-
factured
Articles. The working up of raw materials into a new form received the name of *specificatio;* but it is in fact only a special instance of accession. Here the question at once arose whether the labour or the material was principal. Manifestly the logical idea was of little use, and, after much controversy, the rule was finally settled as follows :—
If any part of the material employed belonged to the workman, the workman was the owner of all ; if not, the question was whether the article could be resolved into its raw material. If it could, the owner of the materials was held to be the owner of the whole ; if not, the workman was the owner. Thus a vessel of gold, silver, or other metal would be the property of the owner of the metal how-

ever exquisite and valuable the workmanship ;
but a person who had made wine out of another's
grapes, or flour out of another's wheat, was the
owner of the product, because it could not be
resolved into its original material. Those rules
applied, however, only when there was something
of workmanship ; if metals, such as gold or silver, *Com-*
were merely fused into one lump, or wheat belong- *mixtio.*
ing to two persons was mixed together, or mead
from one man's wine and another's honey, in all *Confusio.*
such cases the owners of the several parts were
held to be joint-owners of the whole, and no accession took place. Cases of this sort were called
commixtio or *confusio.*

The institution of private property did not extend *Res extra*
to all the material objects of the universe. The *nostrum*
atmosphere, for example, or the ocean, is not sus- *monium.*
ceptible of the exclusive possession that lies at the
foundation of proprietary rights. Other things
might be partially appropriated, and rights falling
short of ownership might be exercised. The whole
of this branch of the law was created by the
Praetors, and such rights as they recognised were
protected by Interdicts.

Res communes were things whereof no one was *Sea-shore.*
owner, and that all men might use. Such were
the air, running water, the sea, and the sea-shore.
The sea-shore extended to the highest point

reached by the waves in winter storms. The right of fishing in the sea belonged to all men. Any one could haul up his nets on the shore, or spread them out to dry, or build a hut for himself. So long as the structure existed it was private property ; but when it fell into ruins the soil again became common. Every one had the right to prevent any construction on the shore that would interfere with his access to the sea or the beach.

Res Publicæ. *Res Publicae* were the property of the Roman people, whereof the use was free to all. The chief examples were public roads, harbours, and rivers, and the banks of rivers. In Rome itself the roads were specially under the jurisdiction of the Curule Aediles. Every river that flowed in summer and winter was public. The banks also, measured to the highest point of the winter flood, could be used by the public for the purpose of landing goods or making

Fishing in Rivers. fast boats to the trees. The right of fishing, like the right of navigation, was free to all.

Res Universitatis were things belonging to a municipality or corporation, the use of which was free, such as race-courses and theatres.

Res sacræ. *Res divini juris* consisted of three classes—*sacrae*, originally devoted to the gods above ; *religiosae*, to the gods, the shades. Under the Christian Empire, *sacrae* meant religious edifices ; and *res religiosae*, any ground consecrated for the reception of the dead. *Res sanctae*, such as the walls of cities, were so called because a capital penalty was fixed for those that violated them.

SECT. II.—PERSONAL SERVITUDES.

Ownership, in the full sense of the term, consists Nature of the most extensive rights to things—rights so of Servi-numerous that they cannot be precisely limited— tudes. rights that endure for ever, and are the subjects of unrestricted alienation. If these rights are limited in duration,—as an estate for life in land—a class emerges, which is differently described in different systems of law. In England a life-interest is gene-rally spoken of as limited ownership: in Rome, a Estates life-interest was not regarded as a form of owner-for Life. ship, but as the antithesis of ownership, as a subtrac-tion from the ownership or a burden upon it—in a word, a servitude. The same term is applied not only to the indefinite use of land—for example, involved in the Roman *ususfructus* or estate for life—but to the class of rights strictly definite, as rights of way, which in English Law are known as easements. According to the Roman jurists, usu-fruct, and other interests like it, are called personal servitudes (*servitutes personarum*), because given to an individual for his enjoyment, and dying with him ; whereas praedial servitudes (*servitutes prae-diorum*) were given to persons only as owners of adjoining land. The distinction is not sound. The true distinction is between indefinite rights, such as usufruct, and single or definite rights, such as a right to draw water, or a right to pour the rain-water from your house on to your neighbour's land. These definite rights to things, called by the jurists praedial servitudes, are not, in the nature of things, praedial : theoretically they need not be confined to owners of neighbouring land ; and in a few rare instances in the Roman Law were not so confined. The English Law has the correct distinction. Easements appendant are comparable to praedial servitudes ; but the same easements may be unconnected with the ownership of land—in which case they are said to be easements in gross.

Incorporeal Things.

This seems the proper place to notice another fallacious distinction introduced by the Roman writers, and followed by their English copyists. Some things, we are told, are corporeal, others incorporeal. Corporeal things can be touched, as a farm, a slave, gold, or wheat. Incorporeal things cannot be touched ; they consist of rights, as an inheritance, usufruct or obligation. This means that the right of inheritance or the right of usufruct is incorporeal. Corporeal things, we are told, can be possessed and delivered ; incorporeal things do not admit of possession or delivery. But with all this subtlety the jurists overlooked the fact that they were making a distinction without a difference. The right of ownership, which was transferred by the delivery of the thing, is just as incorporeal as the right of usufruct. So arbitrary is the division that a life-interest in land is a corporeal thing in English Law, and a life-interest in land was incorporeal in the Roman Law. The meaning is simply that delivery was confined in Roman Law to the transfer of ownership, whereas in English Law the delivery of land might be for an estate for life, or in fee-simple, according to the intention of the parties. The true distinction is between the groups of rights transferred by delivery, and those transferred in other ways; in the Roman Law the first group consisted of ownership only; all other rights to things were transferred in a different manner. By a figure of speech, the rights transferred by delivery were said to constitute corporeal things.

A usufruct is the right of using and taking the *Quasi-* fruits of anything. It was understood to be given *usufruct* for life, unless a shorter period was expressed. It may exist in land, houses, slaves, beasts, and in short everything except what is consumed by use. By a senatus consultum, however, it was determined that a legacy of things consumed by use, such as money, wine, oil, wheat, garments, by way of usufruct, should not be void. On the legatee's giving security to return to the heirs of the testator on his death the articles so bequeathed, or their value in money, they were given to him. Such a legacy was merely a loan without interest. As it bore a certain analogy to usufruct, it was called quasi-usufruct.

Rights of *Fructuarius.*

The usufructuary of land became owner of the crops as soon as they were gathered, but not before. Consequently if he died before that event, the crops belonged to the owner. Generally speaking, but with one exception, the rights of an English tenant for life of land are the same as the rights of the usufructuary. An English tenant may work mines or quarries that have been opened, but cannot open new mines or quarries. The usufructuary was free from this restriction. A usufructuary could not cut timber. Trees overthrown by wind or dead could be taken to repair the house, but not usually for fuel. The usufructuary could, however, take branches to stake his vines, and lop pollards (*silva caedua*).

Usufruct of House.

The usufructuary of a house could use it, but must not alter the character of the building. He was not allowed even to put a roof on bare walls. He could not put up a new building, unless required for strictly agricultural purposes; and he could not pull down any building, even one he had himself put up. Thus we learn where Lord

Coke got his idea that if the life-tenant put up a house, it was waste, and if he pulled it down again, that was double waste.

In ancient times, usufruct was established by a surrender in court (*cessio in jure*), a fictitious suit, which may be compared with the obsolete Fines and Recoveries of English Law. But in the time of Justinian a usufruct was created either by legacy or by agreements and stipulations. The usufruct was extinguished if the usufruct and ownership vested in the same person (*consolidatio*); if the usufructuary neglected to exercise his right for the usual period of prescription; or if the thing perished, or its essential character was altered.

Creation and Extinction of Usufruct.

Use (*usus*) meant use without the fruit. One that had the use of a farm could have only such vegetables, fruits, flowers, etc., etc., as were required for his daily needs. He must not hinder the farm-work. He that had the use of a house could use it for himself and family; it was doubted if he could receive a guest, and he could not transfer his right to another. Use was established or extinguished in the same ways as usufruct.

Usus.

Habitatio (the right of dwelling in a house) and *operae servorum* (use of slaves' services) were distinguished from usufruct by technicalities that need not be noticed.

Habitatio.

*Prae-
rium.*

Precarium was holding land or a moveable at the will of the grantor. This tenure has a certain historical interest. The tenant, although his interest was so slight, had possessory rights protected by interdicts ('Roman Law,' pp. 218-220).

SECT. III.—PRAEDIAL SERVITUDES.

Nature of
a Praedial
Servitude.

A praedial servitude is a definite right of enjoyment of one man's land by the owner of adjoining land. The land in favour of which the right is created is called the *praedium dominans*, that over which it is created is called *praedium serviens*. Servitudes were for the land, in this sense, that the necessities of the dominant land constituted the measure of the enjoyment allowed. A right to lead water to a farm was restricted to the amount of water necessary for the use of that farm. So if the right was to take sand or lime from adjoining land, then no more could be taken than was wanted for the farm to which the right was attached.

General
Maxim.

From the nature of servitude, it followed that an owner could not have a servitude over his own land (*nulli res sua servit*). An owner who, as such, is entitled to every possible use of his land, has no need of a right to one particular mode of enjoyment.

Servitudes
are Nega-
tive or Af-
firmative.

Again, the nature of the duty imposed by a servitude on the owner of the servient land is purely

negative. Except in the case where a man's walls
or pillars were used to support another's building,
where by special agreement the duty to repair
could be cast upon the owner of the walls or
pillars, a positive duty could not be imposed.
(*Servitutum non ea natura est, ut aliquid faciat
quis, sed ut aliquid patiatur, aut non faciat.*) When
the duty laid upon the owner of the servient land
was merely not to do something, as not to shut out
his neighbour's light, the servitude was said to
be *negative;* if it consisted in forbearance, in per-
mitting another to do what but for the servitude
he would not be entitled to do, as, to allow
another to walk across one's land, the servitude
was said to be *affirmative.*

Servitudes were subject to certain other rules of
a technical character. Thus, it was said that all
servitudes ought to be capable of enduring as long
as the land to which they were attached. But exceptions were allowed, and a right of water even
from an artificial reservoir might be granted.
Again, it was said that a servitude was indivisible.
Thus, if the owner of land dies, leaving several
houses, each heir is entitled to the enjoyment of
the servitudes. But perhaps the most technical
rule of all was that there could not be a servitude
of a servitude. Thus, if Titus has a right of leading water over neighbouring farms, these neigh-

*Servitudes
perpetual.*

*Servitudes
Indi-
visible.*

*Servitus
servitutis.*

E

bours cannot have a servitude of drawing water from the aqueduct. But notwithstanding the rule, an agreement to permit them to draw water bound Titus, although it was not a servitude.

Division of Servitudes.
Praedial servitudes were of two kinds, RURAL (*jus rusticorum praediorum*), and URBAN (*jus urbanorum praediorum*). Rural servitudes affect chiefly or only the soil, and could exist if no houses were built; urban servitudes affect chiefly or only houses, and could not exist without houses. That is the correct distinction; for a right-of-way, which is a rural servitude, may exist in a town; and a right to rest a beam or joist on a neighbour's wall, which is an urban servitude, may exist in the country. In ancient times rural servitudes in Italy were *res mancipi*, and could be conveyed only by *mancipatio* or *cessio in jure*; urban servitudes were *res nec mancipi*.

Rights of Way.
Among rural servitudes, the most usual were —(1) Rights of way; *iter*, a right for a man to walk but not to drive a beast or a carriage; *actus*, the right to walk and drive a beast or a carriage; *via*, more extensive, including the right to draw stones and wood and heavy laden waggons. (2)

Rights of Water.
Rights of water included the leading of water through another's land (*aquaeductus*). Usually the water must be conveyed in pipes, although, if so arranged, stone channels might be used. In the

absence of agreement, the quantity of water to be taken was fixed by custom ; but unless by special agreement or by custom the water could not be used for irrigation. *Aquaehaustus* is the right of drawing water from a well or fountain on another man's land. The right of taking cattle to water on another's land was called *pecoris ad aquam appulsus.* Again, one might have the right to put cattle to pasture on the land of another, or to quarry for stones, or to dig for sand or chalk, or to cut stakes for vines, and many similar rights.

Other Rights.

The principal urban servitudes included support to another's building (*oneris ferendi*); inserting beams `(*tigni immittendi*) in the wall of another's house for security, or for covering to a walk along the wall ; the right to refuse, or the obligation to receive, the droppings of water from the tiles of a house (*stillicidium*), or the rain water from a gutter (*flumen*); the right against a neighbour to prevent an increase to the height of his house (*altius non tollendi*) ; the right to prohibit any construction that would shut out light from a house or the general view (*ne luminibus officiatur, et ne prospectui offendatur*); the right of passing a sewer through another's ground.

Urban Servitudes.

A servitude involving a burden upon the ownership of land could of course be created only by owners. An owner could burden his land with a

Creation of Servitudes.

servitude by agreement and stipulation; and such an agreement would be implied if the owner of the dominant land had enjoyed a servitude for the full period of prescription applicable to land. Again, by will an owner could impose the burden of a servitude upon any person to whom he bequeathed the land. Once established, a servitude continued until it was *Extinction of Servitudes.* surrendered by agreement, or merged, when the person to whom a servitude was due became owner of the land upon which the servitude was imposed. In this case, even if the lands were afterwards separated, the servitude was not restored, except by special agreement. If a person entitled to an affirmative servitude did not exercise his right for the period of prescription, he lost it; so, if the person entitled to a negative servitude allowed that period to elapse after the owner of the servient land had violated the servitude, as, for example, by shutting out his lights, without making any complaint, he in like manner lost his right also.

SECT. IV.—EMPHYTEUSIS.

Perpetual Leases. Emphyteusis is a grant of land for ever, or for a long period, on the condition that an annual rent (*canon*) shall be paid to the grantor and his successors, and that, if the rent be not paid, the grant shall be forfeited. This tenure may be

traced to the long or perpetual leases granted by
the Roman State of lands taken in war. The
rent given for such land was called *vectigal,* and
the land itself *ager vectigalis.* The advantages of
this perpetual lease were appreciated by corpora-
tions, ecclesiastical and municipal. A tenure that
relieved the owners from all concern in the management of their lands and gave them in exchange
a perpetual right to rent, seems to be specially
beneficial for corporate bodies. The same tenure
was adopted by private individuals, under the
name of Emphyteusis. In the time of Gaius a
controversy was maintained as to whether Emphyteusis was a sale or letting to hire of land. It
resembled sale, inasmuch as it gave a right for
ever to the land, but it differed from sale in respect
of the price being an annual payment instead of
a sum down. It resembled hire in respect of the
rent ; it differed from hire in respect of the perpetual interest of the tenant. The Emperor Zeno Law of
terminated the discussion, by declaring that the Zeno.
incidents of Emphyteusis should be governed
by the agreement of the parties, and in the
absence of such agreement, that the total destruction of the land or houses should terminate
the tenure, but that for a partial loss the tenant
should have no claim to an abatement of the
rent.

Rights of Emphyteuta. The rights of the tenant (*Emphyteuta*) were almost unrestricted, except that he must not destroy the property so as to impair the security for the rent. The tenant paid all the taxes, and he could be ejected from the land if for three years he failed to pay his rent or produce the receipts for the public burdens. The tenant could sell his right, but was bound to give notice to the owner of the sum offered to him, and the owner had the option of buying it at that amount. If the owner did not exercise his right of pre-emption, the tenant could sell to any fit and proper person without the consent of the owner. The owner was bound to admit the buyer into possession, and was entitled to a fine (*laudemium*) not exceeding two per cent. of the purchase money for his trouble.

SECTION V.—MORTGAGE.

Contractus fiduciae. The earliest mortgage of the Roman Law was an actual conveyance by *mancipatio,* executed by the borrower to the lender, upon an agreement (*contractus fiduciae*) that if the purchase-money were repaid by a day named, the lender would reconvey the property to the borrower. If by the day named the borrower had not paid off the loan, his property was entirely gone. But that was not the worst. The borrower might be willing to repay the money,

but in the meantime the lender might have sold
the property, and the borrower could not follow
it in the hands of the purchaser. This grave
defect of the law it was sought to remedy by
declaring the lender, under these circumstances,
to be infamous. Clamant as these evils were, it
required even a sharper sting of injustice to goad
the praetor into action. It would seem that where
the conveyance was not made by *mancipatio*, even
the solemn promise to return the property on repayment of the loan had no legal effect ; and the
lender could keep the property although its value
might greatly exceed the loan, and refuse to accept
repayment. At this point the praetor interfered,
and issued an edict to the effect that where a
lender got possession of his debtor's property, he
should be compelled to give it up on the debtor *Pignus*
making a tender of the loan. To the borrower he
gave for this purpose an *actio pigneratitia*, and
such an informal pledge was known as *pignus*.
The object of the praetor was merely to redress
a flagrant wrong and prevent an unjust creditor
taking advantage of a mere absence of formality
to rob his debtor of his property; but the result
of his intervention was practically to endow the
Roman law with a simpler and more convenient
form of mortgage. The mere delivery of a thing
was enough to give the creditor full security, while

at the same time the ownership remained with the debtor, and thus the creditor was disabled from fraudulently conveying the property. The creditor, not being owner, could not give a buyer the ownership that he himself did not possess.

Hypotheca. But the *pignus*, although a great improvement, fell short of the requirements of a satisfactory form of mortgage. The creditor did not obtain any security, unless the possession of the property was given to him. Thus, in order to obtain a loan, an owner was subject to the great inconvenience of parting with the possession of his property. In some cases, where a security was desiderated, this condition could not be complied with. Thus when a landlord let a vineyard to a tenant for the usual period of five or seven years, he naturally desired to have a special claim on the stock and implements of the farmer as a security for his rent. But as it was essential these things should remain in the possession of the farmer, the landlord was disabled from enjoying the security of a *pignus*. Some time before Cicero, a praetor of the name of Servius *Actio Serviana.* introduced an action by which he gave the landlord of a farm a right to take possession of the stock of his tenant for rent due, when the tenant had agreed that the stock should be a security for the rent.) The name given to such a security—

hypotheca—points to the Greek origin of this con-
trivance. It was not long, however, before the
advantages of such a security were appreciated in
other cases, and at length the action introduced
by Servius, under the name of *quasi-Serviana*, was
allowed in all cases where an owner retained possession, but agreed that his property should be a
security for a debt. ✓Thus in the result, a mere
agreement, which need not even be in writing,
and without any transfer of possession to the mortgagee, enabled an owner to borrow money and
give ample security to the creditor without subjecting himself to any inconvenience. Practically in
the later Roman law no distinction was made
between *pignus* and *hypotheca.*

If the mortgagee was not in possession, he could Power
sue for the property in the hands of any person of Sale.
possessing it. He could then exercise the power
of sale, which in the Roman law was an inherent
right of the mortgagee. If the parties had agreed
as to the manner, time, etc., of the sale, their agreement was to be observed ; if not, the creditor must
give formal notice of his intention to sell to the
debtor ; and thereafter two years must elapse
before the sale could be made. If the creditor
sold, he must give the surplus, after paying himself, to the debtor. Justinian allowed foreclosure
only when the creditor was unable to find a

Fore-
closure.
buyer at an adequate price. But the debtor must have due notice, and if within a specified time he did not pay, the creditor obtained the ownership on petition to the emperor. Even then a debtor was allowed two years' grace; but if he did not pay all principal and interest within that time, his claim was absolutely foreclosed.

Priority. If the same thing were mortgaged to several persons, and the property was not sufficient to pay them all, the question of preference or priority arose. Except in the case of a small number of privileged mortgages, the question of priority was determined by two principal rules. First, a mortgage made by a public deed, that is a deed prepared by a notary (*tabellio*), and sealed in the presence of witnesses, or even by a private writing signed by three witnesses, was preferred to an earlier mortgage not executed with these solemnities. ' Secondly, unwritten mortgages, or written but unattested by witnesses, took effect according to priority of time. When the same thing was hypothecated at different times to different persons, he that has the first hypothec excludes all others ; in like manner, the second excludes the third, and the third the fourth. But at what moment does a hypothec take effect ? When possession is obtained, or if the debt is future or conditional, when the sum becomes due ? These times were immaterial;

priority was determined by the date when the agreement of mortgage was made.

Usually no hypothec existed except by agree- Implied Mort- ment ; but in some cases the law set up an implied gages. mortgage. Thus at Rome the landlord of a dwelling-house had an hypothec, in the absence of express agreement, over the furniture (*invecta et illata*, *i.e.*, whatever was brought for personal use by the tenant) in the house hired from him, as security for the rent, and for other claims he might have under the tenancy. Justinian extended this law to the provinces. In the case of farms the landlord had an implied hypothec over the crops from the moment they were gathered ; but he had no hypothec over the agricultural implements, cattle, or slaves, or household furniture, except by special agreement.

CHAPTER IV.

THE LAW OF OBLIGATIONS.

SECT. I.—GENERAL PRINCIPLES OF THE LAW OF CONTRACT.

Convey
ance dis-
ting ished
from Con-
tract.

TO determine the true place of contract in a proper classification of law, it is necessary to apprehend, in the first instance, the difference between Conveyance and Contract. Conveyance is the transfer of ownership or of rights partaking of the nature of ownership (rights *in rem*); contract creates obligations or rights *in personam*. A right *in rem* is a right availing against all men generally, and is a right to forbearances ; a right *in personam* is a right availing against a specified individual or specified individuals, and is a right either to acts or to forbearances. The right of a master over his slave is a right *in rem*; it is a right against all men that they shall forbear from depriving the master of the possession or services of his slave. The right of a patron to maintenance from his freedman is a right *in personam*; it is a right against the freedman alone, and it is a right to an act or service. Ownership, again, is an aggregate Rights *in* of rights *in rem*. An owner has a right as against *rem* and *in personam*. all men generally that they shall not deprive him of the possession or use of the thing belonging to him. Contract is the antithesis of ownership. It creates duties binding the promisor or promisors, and no other persons, and those duties are generally to render services, and not merely to exercise forbearances. 'The essence of an *obligatio*,' says the jurist Paul, 'does not consist in this, that it makes a thing ours, or a servitude ours (*jus in rem*), but that it binds another to give something to us or do something for us (*jus in personam*).'

Right and duty are correlative terms. A. can- Right not have a right unless B. or C. owes a duty and Duty Correla- to him. Partly from the circumstance that *jus* tive. rarely meant 'a right,' and that no other Latin term conveniently renders that idea, and partly from the fact that the forms of actions were framed upon an allegation of duty, the Roman jurists did not speak of rights *in personam*, but of the correlative *obligatio*. An obligation was defined to be the legal bond that ties us down to do something according to law. (*Obligatio est juris vinculum, quo necessitate adstringimur alicujus solvendae rei, secundum nostrae civitatis jura.*)

Rights *in personam* (and consequently *obliga-* Contract *tiones*) fall into two classes. Either they arise and Quasi-Contract.

from the consent of the parties, or they are created by law, irrespective of the consent of the parties. The first are contracts, the second, quasi-contracts. The duties of a tutor to a pupil do not arise from any contract between the tutor and pupil, but they belong to the category of '*obligatio*;' and are not infelicitously said to arise *quasi ex contractu*. By the Roman jurists, Delicts. delicts also are placed as a species of '*obligatio*' alongside contract and quasi-contract. It is true that a person committing a delict is under an obligation to compensate the injured party; and thus if we look merely to superficial logical characteristics, a delict may be classed with obligations. But the true nature of delict, as I have elsewhere shown ('Roman Law,' p. xxxvi), is very different; a delict is a violation of a right *in rem*, and ought, having regard to consistency, to be considered under its proper head of rights *in rem*.

Proposal and Acceptance. A contract, then, arises from the agreement of the parties; but what is 'an agreement?' An agreement involves two elements, a proposal and an acceptance. A person makes a proposal when he signifies to another his willingness to do or not to do something, with a view to obtaining the assent of that other to such act or abstinence. The proposal is said to be accepted when the person to whom the proposal is made signifies his assent thereto.* In the chief contract of the Roman Law, the *stipulatio*, the proposal was made not by the promisor but by the promisee. 'Will you give me 100 *aurei?*' 'I will.' Here the question is put by the creditor, and the debtor accepts the proposal by his answer. In order to make a valid agreement, it is necessary that the answer should agree with the terms of the question, in other words, that the proposal made should be accepted, and not something else. Thus, if the proposal is unconditional and the acceptance conditional, or *vice versa*, there is no agreement. So if the proposal is for something to be done on a future day, and the acceptance is for a different day, there is no agreement. So again, if the stipulator asks, 'Will you give me

---

* Such an agreement is a '*conventio.*'

Contractus is a *conventio* to which the law attaches a *juris vinculum.*

Pactum or *pactio* is an agreement not clothed with an action, but available by way of defence to an action. In later times certain pacts (*pacta legitima, pacta praetoria*) were enforced by action, and nevertheless did not obtain the name of *contractus.*

Pollicitatio is a proposal not meant to be accepted ; as, for example, a vow.

Civilis obligatio is based on statute or custom.

Honoraria obligatio is established by the Praetor in the exercise of his jurisdiction.

Naturalis obligatio cannot be enforced by action, but may be used by way of defence or set-off, and will support a mortgage or suretyship.

Stichus or Pamphilus?' and the answer is, 'I will give Stichus,' there is no agreement, because the proposal is disjunctive and the acceptance is not.

The points common to all contracts may be considered under the following heads :—

    I. Consent—Error.
    II. Time, Place, Condition.
    III. Force, Fraud, and Bad Consideration.
    IV. Illegal Promises.
    V. Incapacity to Contract.
    VI. Agency.

Essential Error.

I. CONSENT—ERROR.—The parties to a contract are said to consent when they agree upon the same thing in the same sense. Their intentions can be expressed only through the medium of language. This medium is a source of error. Error is essential (error *in corpore*) when it is such as prevents any agreement being made ; it is non-essential (error *in materia* or *substantia*) when it does not prevent an agreement arising, but may give a right to one of the parties to withdraw from the contract. Essential error is such as prevents the contracting parties from agreeing upon the same thing in the same sense. This may occur in three ways :—(1) I may intend to sell you one slave, you to buy another—as, if I sold Stichus, and you intended to buy Pamphilus, whom you

misnamed Stichus. If both had meant the same
thing, although they knew it by different names,
the contract would have been good. (2) I intend
to let you a farm; you think you are buying it.
Here again, as the understanding affects the nature
of the rights created, the error is fatal, and there is
no contract. (3) I intend to lend money to Cornelius; Julius falsely representing himself to be
Cornelius, gets the money. Here again there is
no contract of loan, as I did not intend to bind
myself to Julius; and Julius may be proceeded
against for theft.

In all other cases error was non-essential, and Non-
the general rule was that non-essential error did Error.
not vitiate the contract. The subject is not free
from difficulty. Savigny, who has examined the
cases very minutely, arrives at the conclusion
that in sale, even non-essential error vitiated the
contract, where the difference between the thing
bought and that which the purchaser intended to
buy was such as to put the one into a different
category of merchandise from the other. Thus,
if I buy a ring, thinking it to be gold when it
is copper, or silver when it is lead, the contract
is void. Again, if I buy wine, and what is sold
is vinegar, or I buy a female slave, and a male
slave is sold, or *vice versa*, the contract is void.

Time.   II. TIME.—When an agreement was made to pay money or do anything on a particular day, performance could not be demanded before that day ; and not even on that day, because the whole. of the day ought to be allowed the debtor for payment at his discretion. So if the payment is to be made in a given year or month, the whole of the year or month must elapse before an action can be brought. If the contract is to be performed within a limited time—say, to build a house in two years —the question arose whether an action could be brought before the whole period had expired, if so much time had elapsed that it was impossible the works could be constructed within the time. Upon this question the Roman jurists were hopelessly divided, but the preponderance of authority seems to favour the view that in such a case the whole time must elapse before an action could be safely brought for breach of contract. If no time was named in the agreement, money promised became due at once ; and other promises must be performed within a reasonable time.

Place of Perform-ance.   PLACE.—If a promise is made to pay at Ephesus, the debtor could not be sued in Rome, without allowing for any advantage he might have in paying at Ephesus. Generally speaking, if a debtor promised to pay or do something at a particular place, the creditor could not demand

performance elsewhere; but the Praetor had a
discretion to allow the creditor to do so, taking
care that the debtor was not put to a disadvantage.
If nothing was said in the contract as to the place
of performance, frequently that was determined by
the nature of the promise. A promise to deliver a
farm must be performed at the farm; a promise to
repair a house must be performed where the house
is. When that indication was wanting, the general
rule was that the creditor could demand performance in the place where he could sue — that is,
within the jurisdiction to which the defendant was
subject. This rule was subject to a certain qualification. A defendant was not obliged to carry a
moveable from the place where it happened to be
at the time fixed for delivery, except at the risk
and cost of the plaintiff, unless he had purposely
caused the moveable to be kept in an inconvenient
place.

CONDITION.—A condition exists when the per- Condition
formance of a promise is made to depend upon defined.
an event *future* and *uncertain*. If the event is
past or present, the obligation is not suspended
at all, but either at once takes effect, or is wholly
nugatory. If a stipulation is made, 'Do you
undertake to give it if Titius was consul, or if
Mævius is alive?' and neither of these is so, the
stipulation is not valid; but if they are so, it is

valid at once. But when an obligation depends
on an event future and uncertain, it remains to be
seen whether the event does or does not happen
before the obligation can arise. The event must
be uncertain as well as future. A promise to pay
money on the death of Titius is a promise that one
day will certainly have to be performed, but the
day itself is uncertain. Consequently, such a
promise was construed as a certain promise to
pay, as an existing obligation, only the time for
performance being uncertain. The jurists called
this *incertus dies,* as distinguished from *con-
ditio.**

**Conditions
in Con-
tracts and
Wills.**
In the Roman Law a somewhat arbitrary line
was drawn between conditions in contracts and

---

* Certain terms continually recur in the Roman Law which
it is expedient that students should know. A notable distinction was drawn between the inception of the obligation
and the time for performance. When an obligation begins
to exist, it was said, *dies cedit;* when performance may be
demanded, it was said *dies venit.* If I agree to give a sum
to Maevius, at one and the same moment the debt exists
(*dies cedit*), and payment may be demanded (*dies venit*). If
I agree to pay Maevius a sum of money a year hence, then
at once the debt exists (*dies cedit*), but payment cannot be
demanded before the end of the year (*dies non venit*). If I
agree to pay a sum to Maevius if the ship 'Flora' arrives
from Carthage, then until that event happens there is no
obligation (*dies non cedit*); but when the event happens, at
once the obligation exists, and performance may be demanded (both *dies cedit* and *dies venit*).

conditions in legacies or wills. Although in a conditional contract the obligation did not exist until the condition was fulfilled, yet, even if the creditor died before the event, his heir got the benefit of the contract if the event afterwards occurred. A conditional promise gave rise to a hope only that there would be a debt, and that hope was transmitted by the creditor to his heir if he died before the event happened. But if a legacy or inheritance were given conditionally, and the legatee or heir died before the event happened, he transmitted nothing to his heir. Again, if the event upon which a promise was made to depend was one that could not or ought not to occur (*i.e.*, was impossible or illegal), then the contract was held to be altogether null and void. But in the case of a will, if a legacy or an inheritance were left subject to an illegal or impossible condition, the legacy or inheritance was held to be validly given, and the condition was simply wholly disregarded. ¹ 'If I touch the sky with my finger,' is a condition physically impossible; 'If you kill Titius, I will give you 100 *aurei*,' is a condition illegal.

Illegal Conditions.

III. FORCE, FRAUD, AND BAD CONSIDERATION.—A promise extorted by fear was not binding. Force (*vis*) is when a promise is made in *Vis.*

Metus. consequence of the actual exercise of superior force. Intimidation (*metus*) is a threat of such present immediate evil as would shake the constancy of a man of ordinary firmness. Whether the force or intimidation was applied by the party benefiting by the promise, or by a third party, the contract was equally void. The effect of fraud *Dolus.* (*dolus*) was somewhat different. If the fraud was perpetrated by one not a party to the contract, the contract was valid, and the remedy of the debtor was by an action for fraud against the person deceiving him. Fraud is a term scarcely admitting precise definition. It may be described and illustrated, but hardly defined. In the widest sense, fraud (*dolus*) means every act or default that is against good conscience. It occurs chiefly in two forms, either the representation as a fact of something that the person making the representation does not believe to be a fact (*suggestio falsi*), or the intentional concealment of a fact by one having knowledge or belief of the fact (*suppressio veri*).

Illustrations.

Titius sells a female slave to Gaius, holding out that she had borne children, when she had not. Titius must submit to a reduction of the price, or to have the slave returned.

Maevius sells a house in Rome without informing the buyer that it was liable to a rate for the support of an aqueduct. Maevius must submit to a reduction of the price.

Gaius sells his slave Stichus, on account of his habit of stealing, and does not inform the buyer of the character of Stichus. Gaius must pay the loss caused by the slave's thefts.

Julius, in treaty for the purchase of a farm, went out with the owner to see it. After the visit, and before the treaty was concluded, a number of trees were blown down by the wind. Julius cannot claim the trees as buyer, because they were severed from the land before the date of the contract ; but if the owner knew, and Julius did not, that the trees had been blown down, the owner must pay the value of the trees.

A vendor knowing that the land is burdened with a servitude, says nothing about it, but makes a clause in the agreement that he will not be answerable for any servitude to which it may turn out that the land is subject. He may nevertheless be sued for the *suppressio veri*.

Titius sells an ox to Gaius. The ox suffers from a contagious disorder that affects and destroys all the cattle of Gaius. If Titius knew that the ox was diseased, he must pay the value of all the cattle of Gaius ; if he did not know, then the price of the ox is to be reduced to the sum Gaius would have given for it if he had known it was diseased.

Although the Roman Law did not generalise the doctrine of valuable consideration, which lies at the root of the English law of contract, yet if a promise were made for an illegal consideration (*injusta* or *turpis causa*) it could not be enforced Again, where a promise was made for an intended consideration, and the consideration failed, there was no obligation. Thus if I gave a written promise to pay 100 *aurei* at the end of six months, in consideration of a sum intended to be lent to me, and no money ever was lent, the promise

Bad Consideration.

could not be enforced. The agreement was said
to be *sine causa.*

IV. Impossible and Illegal Promises.—

Impossibilium nulla obligatio est. A person may
undertake to do what he cannot perform.

Legal Impossibility. That is not impossibility within the meaning
of the maxim. A thing is impossible, within
the meaning of the maxim, when it is something that no human being can do. If I sell a
man, whom I suppose to be my slave, but who
is really free, the contract is one that cannot be
carried out. Again, if I agree to buy what is
really, without my knowledge, my own, the contract is manifestly nugatory. Equally so a contract
dealing with something as private property, which
is not capable of being so dealt with, as a church,
or grave, or theatre, or forum belonging to the
public is void. Such contracts are invalid, even if
afterwards the things dealt with become private
property and capable of being bought and sold. A
sale of a freeman as a slave is not made valid even
if the freeman should afterwards be reduced to
slavery. But in such agreements an important distinction is to be observed. The impossibility of
performing the contract may be known to both
parties to the contract, or only to one of them. If
a person, knowing that he could not perform his

promise, sold a public thing or a freeman to a buyer ignorant of the impossibility, an action for breach of contract, on the ground of deceit, could be successfully maintained against the vendor. The measure of damages was the loss sustained in consequence of the false representation.

Again, a contract was void if it contravened Illegality some statute, or public morality or public policy. A contract to steal, or to commit sacrilege, or to hurt or injure anyone, was void. In the Digest many instances exhibiting the Roman notions of public policy will be found. One alone may be given as an example—the *pactum de quota litis.* This meant an agreement whereby a person undertook to conduct a lawsuit for another, receiving a definite share of the proceeds. This was void, but an agreement to support litigation by a loan for interest was valid.

V. INCAPACITY. — The presumption that an Infants, agreement freely entered into is for the benefit Minors, Madmen. of the parties entirely fails when one of the parties is, by reason of disease or immaturity of mind, incapable of properly judging his own interests. A madman, accordingly, could not bind himself, except during a lucid interval. The case of infants and minors has been already considered (pp. 38, 41).

But, in addition to these grounds of incapacity, Slaves. which occur in all systems of law, the domestic

institutions of the Romans were the cause of special
disabilities. Thus slaves, who had no *locus standi*
in a Roman court, and who had no property, could
not make contracts for themselves. An agreement made by a slave, so far as regards himself,
could not have any higher validity than a mere
naturalis obligatio, upon which he could neither
sue nor be sued. But that broad rule of law
requires qualification. To the extent to which a
slave, by the indulgence of his master, could have
property, to the same extent he had a capacity to
contract, and to bind that property in the hands of
his master. To the extent of his *peculium* a slave
could bind himself where a freeman could do so,
and his master was liable to an action (*actio de
peculio*) to enforce payment. The master had a
right first to deduct all claims he had against his
slave, unless indeed the *peculium* was employed by
the slave, with the knowledge of his master, in
trade. In this case the master ranked merely
as a creditor along with the other creditors of the
slave (*actio tributoria*). The master, again, was not
liable if the slave, without valuable consideration,
undertook to answer for the debt of another.

Persons under the power of a *paterfamilias* were
subject to similar, but not identical, disabilities.

Filii-
familias.
So far as they had separate property, they could
bind themselves by contract ; but if they had no

such property, the rule was that they could be sued personally upon their contracts; but they could not sue their debtors, inasmuch as the benefit, although not the burden, of their contracts accrued to their *paterfamilias*.

VI. AGENCY.—An all-pervading, all-important conception of modern law is Agency or Representation, by which the power of creating legal obligations can be almost indefinitely multiplied. The early Roman Law admitted agency in not a single department, neither in lawsuits, nor in the conveyance of property, nor in the making of contracts. The actual person who intervened in a legal act could benefit by it, and no other. This is to be connected with the strict Formalism of the old law. Every legal act involved elaborate ceremonies, and possessed in the eyes of the Romans a species of sacramental efficacy. It appears to have been absolutely inconceivable to them that the benefit of these forms could be given to a person that had not recited the solemn words, nor partaken in their ceremonies. *Agency unknown to Early Law.*

A perfect type of agency implies three things: (1) that the authority of the agent is derived from the consent of the principal; (2) that the agent can neither sue nor be sued in respect of the contracts he makes on behalf of his principal; and *Perfect Agency.*

(3) that the principal alone can sue or be sued.
Agency rests upon the authority given by the
principal, and it is more or less imperfect, unless
the agent is wholly irresponsible, and the principal
alone can sue and be sued.   The agent does his
work most completely when, as soon as the transaction is complete, he drops out of view, and the
principal and third party are brought face to face.

*Acquisi-
tion by
those
alieni
juris.*

The old law, although it recognised no representation of one free man by another, possessed
in the ancient constitution of the family no contemptible substitute.   Slaves, sons, and others
under the power of a *paterfamilias* could acquire
for him, or rather they could acquire only for him
and not for themselves. This was not agency—
for the slave could acquire for the master not
merely without his consent, but in opposition to
his express command—but so far it served practically the same purpose as agency. The slave,
however, could not subject his master to any
burdens. 'Our slaves can better our condition,
but cannot make it worse.' Thus the slave could
act only in unilateral engagements : he could
not buy or sell, or make any other contract
involving reciprocal duties between the parties.
This defect was, however, remedied by the
Praetor, who gave an action (*actio quod jussu*)
against the *paterfamilias* where, by his express

authority, the son or slave had made a contract
with a third party. He even went further, and
gave an action against the *paterfamilias* when,
without express authority, the son or slave had
made a contract for the benefit of the master's
property (*actio de in rem verso*). This included
all necessary or beneficial expenditure ; such as
cultivating the master's land, repairing his house,
clothing slaves, or paying the master's debts. The
ratification of the *paterfamilias* was not necessary ;
for the son or slave had, in virtue of the Praetorian
action, an implied authority to make contracts for
the benefit of his estate. The result, therefore, of
the old principle of the civil law, eked out by the
Praetor's actions, was, that sons or slaves under the
power of a *paterfamilias* could act as agents for
him, but not for any other person.

In two instances where the necessities of com-
merce made themselves felt, an approach was
made to agency in the case of free persons as
well as of slaves and others *in potestate*. (1) The
owner or charterer of a vessel (*exercitor*) was
bound by all contracts made by the captain of
the ship relating to the ship, its seaworthiness
and freight. The authority of the captain went
to that extent, unless it were limited by his instructions. The captain was personally liable
upon his contracts, as well as the owner, and

in this respect did not enjoy the immunity of a true agent. Again, the owner could not sue the third parties directly; he had no direct remedy, except against his own agent; and thus his rights fell short of those of a true principal.

Shopmen as Agents. (2) A servant or manager of a shop or business (*institor*) could bind his principal by all contracts made in relation to the business. Here again, however, the servant or manager was himself liable personally for his contracts; and, as a general rule, the principal could not sue the debtors of his manager, but could only require his manager to transfer his rights of action. In extreme cases, however, where it was necessary to avoid loss, the principal could, by leave of the Praetor, sue third parties directly. In a few cases, not strictly falling within the description of the *institoria actio*, a principal was allowed to sue directly persons who had made contracts with his agents. But beyond that the Roman Law did not go in establishing a law of agency for contracts. Savigny's Views. Savigny, whose opinion carries deservedly great weight, is of a different opinion. He thinks that in the later law agency was universally admitted in non-formal contracts. The arguments that seem to me fatal to this view are discussed at length in 'Roman Law' (pp. 441, 442).

SECT. II.—CLASSIFICATION OF CONTRACTS.

Contracts are divided in the Institutes of Gaius and of Justinian into four classes, according to the manner in which they are made : (1) by acts (*re*); (2) by words (*verbis*); (3) by writing (*literis*); and (4) by consent. This division is faulty; it is not quite accurate, and it does not divide the classes according to their most important characters. To prevent mistakes, it will be convenient to place in parallel columns the contracts as arranged in the Institutes, and in the order here followed. Those enclosed in brackets were obsolete in the time of Justinian.

IN THE INSTITUTES.

A. Contracts *re*.
1. Mutuum.
2. Commodatum.
3. Deposit.
4. Pignus.

B. Contracts *verbis*.
1. Stipulatio.

C. Contracts *literis*.
1. [Expensilatio].
2. [Chirographa].
3. [Syngraphae].

D. Contracts *consensu*.

1. Sale.
2. Hire.
3. Partnership.
4. Mandate.

REARRANGEMENT.

A. Formal Contracts.
1. [Nexum].
2. Stipulatio.
3. [Expensilatio].
4. [Chirographa].
5. [Syngraphae].

B. Contracts based on Part Performance.
1. Mutuum.
2. Commodatum.
3. Deposit.
4. Mandate.

C. Contracts for valuable consideration.
1. Sale.
2. Hire.
3. Partnership.

English
and Ro-
man Prin-
ciples of
Contract.

The principles upon which this arrangement is
made, and the historical relations of the several
contracts, are considered at length elsewhere.
('Roman Law,' p. 353, *sq.*) ·For the English
student, it is necessary to be on his guard against
being misled by the Roman arrangement to over-
look the analogies, more important than the differ-
ences, between the English and Roman Law. At
the first blush, no two systems can appear more
at variance. The English Law does not enforce
gratuitous promises, or, in technical language, promises made without valuable consideration. The
exception is the Formal contract of the English
Law—the Deed, by which is meant a writing,
sealed and delivered. Thus a contract, to be binding, must in England be made by deed, or be supported by a valuable consideration. But the very
idea of 'valuable consideration' seems at first
sight wholly wanting in Roman Law. It does
not appear in Justinian's classification, and in truth
although in some cases a valuable consideration
was essential to a contract, yet the Romans did
not perceive the fact, and fell short of a generalisa-
tion that would have assisted them marvellously
to clear up the confusion that darkens their
system of contract. The Romans started, we
need scarcely with our present knowledge hesitate
to affirm, with only formal contracts; that is, con-

tracts in which the legal validity of the promise Formalism.
depended upon the observance of certain forms
and ceremonies. Formalism triumphed in contract as in every other department of Roman Law.
But the progress of Roman Jurisprudence depended upon the skill with which the jurists were
able to liberate transactions from the trammels of
form.

The chief direction taken by their beneficent Part Performance
industry was to lay hold of the principle known,
to English Equity by the name of Part Performance. Where the law requires a certain form to
be observed, and an agreement is made by parties
without regard to that form, courts of law would
not feel called upon to aid their negligence. But if
one of the parties, on the faith of the agreement,
has done all that he undertook to do, the other
party cannot, without something very like fraud,
accept such performance, and yet refuse to carry
out his part of the agreement. This idea applied at first in a few glaring instances (*mutuum,
depositum, commodatum*), was ultimately adopted
in the widest generality; and it was laid down
that where in a bilateral agreement one of the
parties had performed what he had undertaken,
the other party could be compelled also to perform his part by an *actio in factum praescriptis
verbis*. Such contracts, having no special name,

Innomi-
nate
Contracts.
were said to be innominate. They are compre-
hended in the well-known *formula* of Paul. 'Either,
he says, I give something to you in order that you
may give something to me, or I give something
to you in order that you may do something for
me; or I do something to you in order that you
may give something to me, or I do something
to you that you may do something for me.' (*Do
tibi ut des; do ut facias; facio ut des; facio ut
facias.*)

When this result was attained, the Roman Law
had achieved a great advance, but it still fell short
of the English Law; for unless one of the parties
had actually performed his engagements, the contract could not be enforced at the instance of
either. In the case of sale, hire, and partnership,
a valuable consideration was of the essence of the
contract.

Pacta
Praetoria.
At this point, strictly speaking, the contracts of
the Roman Law are ended. There remains to be
noticed the class of PACTS. The Romans were
fortunate at one time in the possession of two
words, which sharply distinguished agreements
enforceable by law (*contractus*) from agreements
that did not support actions (*pacta*). But in two
instances the Praetors, and in two others, certain
Emperors gave actions to enforce pacts. Those
introduced by the Praetor (*Pacta Praetoria*) were

hypotheca, already considered (p. 72), and the *Legitima Pacta.* *pactum de constituto,* to be hereafter explained. Theodosius and Valentinian enacted that a mere agreement to give a dowry should be binding without any *stipulatio.* Thus the *pactum de constituenda dote* supported an action. Again, Justinian sanctioned the greatest change of all—that a mere promise to give without any consideration ✓ (*pactum donationis*) should be enforceable by action. This decision, so strangely at variance with the traditions of Roman law and the principles of general jurisprudence, was dictated by the growing desire of the clergy to encourage gifts to religious persons or for pious uses. These imperial pacts were called *pacta legitima.*

Except in those instances, the term *pactum* was *Nudum Pactum.* strictly applied to an agreement not enforceable by action. But from an early period the Praetors allowed such agreements to be used by way of defence. (*Nuda pactio obligationem non parit, sed parit exceptionem.*) In English text-books this maxim is often quoted, but in an entirely different sense. In English Law, *nuda pactio* means an agreement not supported by valuable consideration, an idea which, as we have seen, the Romans did not attain to.

An agreement that could not be enforced by *Naturalis obligatio.* action, if it was recognised by law for any purpose, created a *naturalis obligatio*. No action could be maintained upon a mere natural obligation; but it was available by way of defence or set off; if it was voluntarily performed, the debtor could not demand back his money on the ground that it was not due, and was paid by mistake. Again, if a person became surety for a *naturalis debitor*, he could be sued as surety, although the principal debtor could not be sued. A *naturalis obligatio* also was sufficient to support a mortgage; and it could be the foundation of a novation.

SECT. III.—FORMAL CONTRACTS.

Nexum.   The form of *mancipatio*, so extensively employed in the transfer of proprietary rights, was in certain cases, under the name of *Nexum*, employed as a mode of creating contractual obligations.   In what cases it was used we do not certainly know, but it seems to have been narrow in its application.   It was obsolete long before the time of Justinian.

Stipulatio.   The *Stipulatio* was the chief Formal Contract. It may be traced back to a hoary antiquity; it survived in full vigour to the dissolution of the Roman Empire. It was a verbal contract, and its peculiarity—its form—consisted merely in this, that the promise made must be in answer to a question. ‘Do you promise to give 10 *aurei?*’

'I promise,'—constituted a binding contract. 'I promise to pay you 10 *aurei*' created no legal obligation whatever. In later times this was all the formality required. The words used might be in any language understood by the parties; the answer need not follow the precise terms of the question if there was substantial agreement. The *stipulator* was he that asked the question; the promiser (*reus promittendo*) was the person bound by the answer. Thus to stipulate, in the Roman Law, does not mean to make a promise, but to ask for a promise ; the stipulator was always the creditor. Although the validity of a stipulation depended upon its being made orally, there was nothing to prevent, and much to recommend, the practice of recording the terms of the stipulation in writing. The Roman Law established two legal presumptions in favour of such a writing—(1) that it afforded *prima facie* proof that the parties were present ; and (2) conclusive evidence that the form of question and answer had been observed. The two weak points in the stipulation—the treacherous character of memory and all disputes as to the observance of the proper form of question and answer—were thus fortified. On the other hand, as the *stipulatio* was a contract necessarily unilateral, it was not adapted for agreements involving reciprocal promises ; but the parties

Stipulations reduced to Writing.

might invert the rôle, and make reciprocal stipulations.

Cautio.   In the time of Justinian there existed no contract
made by the form of writing. A written acknow-
ledgment of the receipt of money and of an obligation to repay (*cautio*) was in use, but it was not
a literal contract. It was merely evidence of the
existence of a debt, although evidence which, after
the statutory period of two years, could not be
called in question. During the Republic there
Expen-   existed a true literal contract, made by an entry
silatio.   (*nomen transcriptitium*) in the account books
(*codex*) of the creditor. The *codex* was passing
Chiro-   into oblivion in the time of Cicero, and was super-
grapha.   seded by the *chirographum*, a writing signed by the
Syngra-
phae.   debtor only ; or *syngrapha*, a writing signed by both
debtor and creditor. These forms of contract, as
their names indicate, were of Greek origin. They
were known as early as the second Punic War
(B.C. 210), and maintained their existence down
until the Empire.

Sect. III.—Part Performance.

Contracts   In the contracts said to be made (*re*) by acts,
re.   the legal obligation depended not upon the observance of any forms, but upon the fact that the
plaintiff had performed his part of the contract.
   Mutuum was the giving of any *res fungibiles* to

another as his property, with the intention that at *Mutuum.*
some future time we shall have returned to us, not
the same things, but others of the same nature and
quality. *Res fungibiles* are things dealt with by
weight, number, or measure, as silver, gold, bronze,
money, corn, wine, oil. *Mutuum* was thus a
gratuitous loan.) It carried no interest, unless an
independent obligation was created by *stipulatio*
for that purpose. A promise to lend could not be
enforced ; but if the things were actually lent, it
would have been manifestly unjust not to compel
the debtor to repay according to his promise.

Pecunia trajectitia was a commercial loan, par- Insurance.
taking of the nature of insurance. It was money
lent to buy merchandise, to be shipped at the risk
of the lender, until the goods arrived at the port of
destination.

By a statute passed in the reign of Claudius or Loans to
Vespasian (*Senatus Consultum Macedonianum*), an Sons.
action was refused to any person lending money to
a son in his father's power, even if the contract
was to repay only on his father's death, unless it
was made to procure necessaries.

Commodatum was the gratuitous loan of any- *Commo-*
thing not consumed in the use, and was thus the *datum.*
complement of *mutuum*—the loan of things consumed by use. As a return for the gratuitous benefit Duties
of the loan, the borrower was bound to take all of Borrower.

reasonable care (*exacta diligentia*) of the thing lent —that is, such care as would be taken by a prudent man, and not merely such care as the borrower was accustomed to take of his own goods. If, however, the borrower used the thing in a different way from that bargained for, he was liable if the thing was lost, even without his fault ; and might, indeed, expose himself to an action for theft. Thus, if Titius borrows plate from Gaius to use at supper,

Duties of Lender. and takes it on a journey, and it is stolen by robbers, he is liable to repay it. The lender, on his part, having once given the thing to the borrower, but not before, is bound to suffer the borrower to enjoy the use of the thing according to the terms of the agreement ; and he must pay extraordinary expenses to which the borrower may be put. The lender must pay the money spent on a sick slave, or to catch a runaway slave ; the borrower paid for food, and even medical expenses, if they were slight in amount. Although the contract was gratuitous, yet good faith required that the lender should not knowingly give things for a use for which they were unsuited. If a man lent vessels to hold wine or oil, knowing that they leaked or would spoil the liquor, he was required to pay the value of the oil or wine thereby destroyed.

Deposit. *Depositum* was a contract in which a person agreed to keep a thing for another gratuitously,

and to return it on demand. The receiver was not
allowed to use it, and for that reason he was
not answerable for negligence, but only for fraud.
The depositee might, however, if he pleased, agree
to answer for negligence as well. When a thing
was deposited with a person under distress, as from
a riot, or fire, or fall of a house, or shipwreck, the
depositee, if he proved false to his trust, was liable
like a thief to an action for double the value of the
goods deposited. Such a deposit was said to be
miserabile or *necessarium.*

Pignus was reckoned by the jurists in the class *Pignus.*
of contracts. It has already been described under
the head of Mortgage (p. 71).

Mandatum is not reckoned among contracts *re* Mandate.
in the Institutes, but on principle it really belongs
to that category.—('Roman Law,' pp. 309, 311, 312,
315.) Mandate is a contract in which one person
(*is qui mandatum suscipit, mandatarius*) promises to
do or to give something, without remuneration, at
the request of another (*mandans* or *mandator*), who,
on his part, undertakes to save him harmless from
all loss. A mandate might be for the benefit of For good
the *mandans* or of a third person, but not exclu- of Manda-
tory alone.
sively, say the Institutes, for the *mandatarius* himself. Thus if Titius advised Gaius to invest his
money in land, rather than to put it out at interest,
and Gaius, acting on the advice, lost by the invest-

ment, he had no claim for an indemnity against Titius. Justinian says this is a piece of advice that Gaius was free to accept or not, rather than a mandate. The decision in this case is right, although the ground upon which it is put is not quite satisfactory. The true question is whether Gaius acted at the request of Titius, and Titius, in consideration of his doing so, promised him an indemnity. It would be contrary to common sense to suppose in such a case that Titius meant to indemnify him. When a man at the request of another acted for the benefit of some other person, it was reasonable to infer a promise of indemnity; but where a man was advised to do something solely for his own benefit, such an inference would be unreasonable. Nevertheless, if in such a case a person expressly promised an indemnity, a contract of mandate was established.

Examples of Mandate.

A mandate might be for the sake of the mandator, as when a man gives you a mandate to manage his business, or to buy a farm for him, or to become surety for him. It might be for the sake of a third person only, as when a man gives you a mandate to manage the business of Titius, or to buy a farm for him, or become surety for him, or lend him money without interest. It might be for the sake of the *mandatarius* and a third person, as when a mandate is given you to lend money to

Titius at interest. It may be for the sake of the mandator and a third person, as when a man gives you a mandate to act in business common to himself and Titius, or to buy a farm for himself and Titius, or to become surety for him and Titius. It may be again for the benefit of the mandator and the *mandatarius*, as when a man gives you a mandate to lend money to Titius for the good of the mandator's property; or, when you wish to bring an action against him as surety, gives you a mandate to bring the action against the principal at his risk. In all those and similar cases, where some person other than the *mandatarius* had an interest in the performance of the contract, it was considered that the request by the mandator implied a promise of indemnity, if the *mandatarius* should suffer any loss by acting upon the request.

The duties imposed upon the *mandatarius* may be reckoned as four.

(1.) He must do what he undertakes. This duty was not, however, absolute. He might renounce the mandate, provided there was time for the mandator to act himself. If I undertake to go to an auction to bid for a farm for another, by giving reasonable notice before the auction I can relieve myself of the obligation. It must be borne in mind that the *mandatarius* acted gratuitously;

Renunciation of Mandate.

if pay was promised to him, he could not withdraw. Again, at the last moment, a *mandatarius*
was excused from performing his engagement for
good reason shown, as if he were suddenly taken
ill, or compelled to leave home on business, or if
the mandator became insolvent, or a bad feeling
arose between the mandator and *mandatarius*. If
the *mandatarius* failed without sufficient reason to
perform his promise, he was made liable in damages, on the ground that the mandator had in consequence of the promise of the *mandatarius* not
done something he would otherwise have done,
and had thereby incurred loss.

Perform-
ance of
Mandate.

(2.) The *mandatarius* must conform to his instructions, on pain of forfeiting his indemnity, and
exposing himself to an action for damages for any
loss falling on the mandator. Many nice questions
arose as to what constituted a substantial fulfil-
ment of a mandate which did not comply with its
literal terms. It was settled by Justinian that if
a mandate were given to buy a farm for 100 *aurei*,
and 110 were given, the *mandatarius* could compel
the mandator to take it off his hands at 100. Of
course a mandate to buy at 100 was fulfilled by
buying at a less sum. A mandate to buy a farm
was considered fulfilled by the purchase of one-
half of it, unless the mandator expressly stated
that he would accept nothing less than the whole

(3.) A *mandatarius* must take as much care of any property he receives as a man of ordinary prudence. This forms a remarkable contrast to the contract of deposit, which like mandate, was gratuitous; and is an exception to the general rule that a gratuitous promisor is liable only for wilful default. This rule, it is not surprising, was not reached without a conflict of opinion. Diligence.

(4.) The *mandatarius* must give up to the mandator everything he gains by the performance of the mandate, and all rights of action acquired against third parties, and must permit the mandator to sue in his name. In this circuitous way the mandator was brought into relation with the third parties with whom contracts were made at his request ; if he could have passed by the *mandatarius* and directly sued such parties as principal, the Romans would have enjoyed a true law of agency. In the absence of such, the contract of mandate afforded no contemptible substitute.

The duties of the mandator are—(1) to pay the *mandatarius* what he has properly expended in executing the mandate ; (2) to accept what the *mandatarius* has bought, and to indemnify him against all obligations that he has incurred by an execution of the mandate. As the *mandatarius* was to gain nothing, so he ought to lose nothing, if he properly performed the mandate. Duties of Mandator.

Termina-
tion of
Mandate.   A mandate might be revoked, or, as we have seen, renounced. It was also put an end to by the death of either mandator or *mandatarius*, subject to this qualification, that if the *mandatarius*, in ignorance of the death of the mandator, carried out the mandate, he was entitled to indemnification. It was not considered right that unavoidable ignorance should bring loss to the *mandatarius*.

SECT. V.—SALE (*Emptio-Venditio*).

Sale how
formed.   Sale is a contract in which one person agrees to give to another for a price the undisturbed possession of anything. This agreement might be made by the parties, if present together, or by letter. [It was held binding as soon as the subject-matter of the sale and the price were determined.] Writing was not essential to the validity of the contract; but if it was contemplated by the parties that the negotiations for a sale should be finally reduced to writing, Justinian somewhat modified the law. He enacted that either party might withdraw before the contract was written out. If the instrument was not written by the parties, it must be signed by the parties. If it was to be drawn up by a notary (*tabellio*), the contract was not complete until the documents were fully finished in every part. These rules did not apply if earnest

(*arrhae*) was given to bind the bargain. If the buyer refused to proceed, he forfeited the earnest-money ; if the vendor, he had to restore the earnest, and its equivalent in value.

There must be a real price, and it must be coined The Price. money, and no other species of valuable considera-tion. If a thing were sold for a nominal price, which the vendor did not mean to exact, there was no sale. Mere inadequacy of price did not vitiate the contract, unless it fell short of half the value, in which case, under a constitution of the Emperors Diocletian and Maximian, the vendor could re-fuse to carry out the contract. It is a moot point whether, if the price were twice as much as the value, the buyer had a similar right to throw up the contract. If no price were fixed by the parties, but they agreed to allow a third person to determine the price, then if that person fixed a price, the contract was complete; but if he did not, the sale went for nothing, as if no price had been determined upon.

In the definition of the contract, it is said that *Varua* *Possessio.* the vendor agreed to give the undisturbed posses-sion (*tradere vacuam possessionem*), which is to be distinguished from ownership. A man had un-disturbed possession when he was actually, by him-self or his representative, in physical possession, and when no one was in a position to eject him by an interdict. I have elsewhere shown (' Roman Law,' p. 199, *sq.*) that possession of this kind was practically ownership,—the only form of ownership permitted by the Roman Law to persons who were not Roman citizens. In this circumstance is to be found the clue to the distinctive peculiarity, and, it may be added, distinctive anomaly, of the Roman law of sale. ⌊The real object of every sale, in Rome as in other parts of the world, was to give the ownership of the thing sold to the buyer, and yet a contract in Rome by a vendor to transfer the ownership of a thing (as distinguished from possession) for a fixed price, was held *not* to be a contract of sale.⌋ The Romans accomplished the true end of sale by means that appear singularly cumbrous and inefficient. The vendor was bound actually to give undisturbed possession, and he was bound also to warrant against eviction, that is, to compensate the buyer in the event of his being evicted by law from a part or the whole of the thing sold, for any ground (*causa evictionis*) existing at the time of the sale. The duty to transfer the ownership is thus split up into two parts, which together are not quite equal to the whole,—the duty to give present possession, and to give compensation in the event of future disturbance. The parts were not equal to the whole, because a buyer might be compelled to accept a property with a defective

Warranty against Eviction.

title, and before the eviction took place, the vendor might be bankrupt or dead, and an action against him for compensation be wholly worthless.) But the Romans were content with this imperfection, for an all-sufficient reason. [It was the only means whereby the law of sale could be opened to persons not citizens—the same cause to which is to be ascribed nearly all the profound changes in the form and spirit of the ancient laws of Rome.

The effect of a completed contract of sale was not to transfer the possession to the buyer, but to give the buyer a right to require the possession to be transferred. In the language of jurisprudence, it gave the buyer a right *in personam* as against the vendor, but no right *in rem* to the thing as against any other person.\ If the vendor, in breach of his contract, transferred the thing to another, the buyer could sue him for damages, but he could not recover the thing itself. [Nor did the delivery even of the possession, in the case where the vendor was owner, vest the ownership in the buyer. The buyer became owner only when he had paid the price, unless the vendor had waived his right to payment, and given the buyer credit.\ In that case the buyer acquired the ownership as soon as the thing was delivered to him.

Delivery of thing sold.

[After the contract of sale, and prior to delivery, it was the duty of the vendor to take good care of

Periculum rei.

the thing sold, but the profit and risk arising from
it were with the buyer. | The interest of the buyer
as owner thus really dated from the time of the
contract of sale. If a mare foaled after the contract, the foal belonged to the buyer; if an inheritance were left to a slave after the price was fixed,
the buyer had the benefit of it. | On the other
hand, if the property were accidentally destroyed or
injured the loss fell upon the buyer, and the vendor
was entitled to the full price. |

Except *res fung.biles.* |In three cases, however, the risk remained with
the vendor. (1.) Things sold by number, weight,
or measure remained at the risk of the vendor,|
until they were set apart, numbered, weighed, or
measured respectively. The risk, however, was
thrown on the buyer if these things were sold in
lots (*per aversionem*), as, for example, 'all that lot
of corn, or oil, or wine.' This was in fact the same
as the sale of specific ascertained goods. (2.) If
Except Condi-tional Sale. the sale were conditional, the rule was more complex. Of course, if the conditions were not ful-
filled, there was no sale, and all loss or damage fell
on the seller. If the conditions were fulfilled, but
before that event the thing was destroyed or
damaged, the rule was that a total loss fell on the
seller, and a partial loss on the buyer. The reason
was that, if the thing perished, the seller was not in
a position to deliver anything to the buyer when

the condition happened and the obligation took effect; but if he could deliver the thing, although damaged or mutilated, he acquitted himself of his promise. (3.) If the agreement were that the buyer had the choice of two things, and one perished, he took the other; but if both perished, the loss fell upon him, and he had to pay the price.

Except Alterna- tive Sale

If the vendor did not deliver at the time he ought, he was responsible not merely for negligence, but for accidental loss. On the other hand, if the buyer did not remove the goods at the time he ought, the vendor was answerable only for wilful misconduct, or extremely gross negligence.

Mora.

The duties of the vendor are these:—(1) To deliver undisturbed possession; (2) to warrant against eviction; (3) prior to delivery to take the same care of the thing (*exacta diligentia*) as a good *paterfamilias.* There remains another and characteristic obligation, (4) the seller must suffer the sale to be rescinded, or give compensation, in the option of the buyer, if the thing sold has undisclosed faults that interfere with the proper enjoyment of it. This duty depended upon the edict of the Curule Aedile, a magistrate who, amongst other functions, was charged with the superintendence of markets. His edict in terms applies only to slaves and animals, but its principle was extended to moveables and even to immoveables. In

Duties of Vendor.

Warranty against Secret Faults.

the case of slaves, the edict applied if the slave had any disease or vice, or was in the habit of wandering (*erro*), or was given to running away (*fugitivus*), or if he had committed a delict or a capital crime, or had attempted suicide, or been sent to the amphitheatre to fight with wild beasts as a punishment; unless any fault of that description was told to the buyer, he had the option of rescinding the sale (*actio redhibitoria*) within six months, or of keeping the slave and demanding a deduction from the price within a year (*actio aestimatoria seu quanti minoris*). In the case of animals, every disease or vice, as biting or kicking in a horse, or a disposition to gore in an ox, had to be disclosed. By analogy it was held that on the sale of a ship there was an implied warranty of soundness, and generally that when an instrument was sold for a purpose, it was not so defective as to be unfit for that purpose. The buyer of land that produced poisonous herbs or grass, could rescind the sale, unless the fault had been disclosed to him.

English Law.

[The rule of the Roman Law is exactly the reverse of that embodied in the maxim '*caveat emptor.*' If both buyer and vendor were ignorant of a fault, the loss fell in Rome on the vendor, in England on the buyer.\ The origin of the Roman rule is to be sought in the slave market. The faults of slaves were known to their owners, but could easily be concealed from buyers. It would have been a serious impediment to business if it had been as dangerous to buy a slave in Rome as a horse in England. Accordingly, long before the edict of the Aedile, a practice grew up of requiring from the vendors of slaves and cattle formal guarantees expressed in stipulations; and the Aedile simply extended that idea by creating an implied warranty against all serious faults that were not expressly disclosed at the time of the sale.

The duties of the buyer in a contract of sale were simple. He must pay the price, he must accept delivery of the goods, and he must pay the expenses the vendor incurs in keeping the thing prior to delivery. *Duties of Buyer.*

SECT. VI.—HIRE (*Locatio-conductio*).

Hire (*locatio-conductio*) is a contract in which one person (*locator*) agrees to give to another (*conductor*) the use of something, or to do some work, in return for a fixed sum. This contract is analogous to, but distinguishable from, several other contracts. It agrees with *commodatum* in being a contract for the use of a thing; but *commodatum* is gratuitous, hire is for a price. If a deposit is made gratuitously, or a service is to be *Hire defined.* *Distinguished from other Contracts.*

Hire distinguished from other Contracts.

rendered gratuitously, the contract is either deposit or mandate; but if payment is to be given, it is *locatio-conductio.* Again, if there be a valuable consideration other than money, the contract is not *locatio-conductio.* If, for instance, a man has an ox, and his neighbour too has one, and they mutually agree that each shall lend the other his ox free ten days in turn, then it is not a *locatio-conductio;* but if one has lent his ox, he can claim the use of his neighbour's ox upon the ground of part performance by the *actio in factum praescriptis verbis.* Although hire is very distinct from sale, yet there were cases in which a difficulty arose. If Titius agrees with a goldsmith that the goldsmith shall, out of his own gold, make rings, and receive 10 *aurei,* it was disputed whether this was a contract of sale or of hire. One view was that it was a compound contract—of sale as regards the material—and of hire, as regards the services of the goldsmith. But it was finally settled that where the workman supplied the material, it was a simple contract of sale; if he supplied only labour, it was a contract of hire.

Hire of Things.

The contract of hire relates to land and other things, or to services. And first of the hire of things.

Tenant had no Right in rem.

A tenant of a house or farm in the Roman Law had no right *in rem* to the subject, but only a right *in personam* against the landlord. In other words, if evicted by his landlord or even by a stranger, he could not invoke the aid of the interdicts by which possession was restored; he could only bring an action for damages against his landlord for breach of contract. The landlord could alone sue the disturbers, but if he failed to do so, he committed a breach of contract.—(' Roman Law,' pp. 210, 334.)

The duties of the landlord (*locator*) were— (1.) To deliver the thing to the tenant (*conductor*), and permit him to keep it for the time agreed upon. If the landlord by his own fault deprived the tenant of his holding before the end of the lease, he must pay full compensation (*id quod interest*); but if the tenant was evicted through no fault of the landlord, the tenant could claim only a remission of the rent, and not damages. Thus if the house was burned down, or the thing let was carried off by robbers, or the farm was confiscated, the tenant was released from rent, but was not entitled to compensation. (2.) The landlord was bound to keep the thing in such a state that the hirer could enjoy the use agreed upon. If the thing deteriorated and was not repaired, the tenant could demand a reduction of the rent, or a release from the contract. Trifling repairs were to be executed by the hirer. (3.) The landlord was responsible if the thing let had such faults as were

Duties of Landlord

Landlord bound to Repair.

Warranty of Fitness

likely to cause damage. If a landlord let a farm, along with the vats or jars used in wine-making, and the vats were rotten, and the tenant lost his wine, the landlord must pay the value of the wine.

Removal of Fixtures. (4.) The landlord must permit the tenant to carry away not only moveables but even fixtures placed by the tenant, provided the tenant did not injure the house. A tenant of land was entitled to com-

Unexhausted Improvements. pensation for unexhausted improvements, except such as he had specially agreed to execute in consideration of a lower rent. The measure of compensation was the increased value of the land.

Duties of Tenant. The tenant was bound—(1.) To pay the rent, with interest if it was in arrear. If rent of a house or farm were in arrear for two years, the tenant could be evicted. In certain cases the landlord was obliged to remit the whole or a part of the rent on account of loss or damage to the crops.—(' Roman Law,' p. 337.) (2.) The tenant must occupy during the term agreed upon, or at all events pay the rent. (3.) The tenant or hirer must exercise due care. He was responsible if the thing was stolen, but not if it was carried away by robbers. (4.) The tenant or hirer must give up the thing upon the expiration of the term agreed upon.

Hire of Services. In the hire of services the jurists, misled by a false analogy, fell into confusion. The hirer pays

the price, the letter gives his services. If the services were not rendered in respect of a particular thing, as the services of a messenger or secretary or domestic servant, the employer was correctly described as *conductor operarum*, and the servant as *locator operarum*. But if the work was to be done in respect of a particular thing, as by a jeweller, or builder, or tailor, or carrier of goods, the jurists called the employer the *locator operis*— that is, of the thing to be worked upon—and the workman the *conductor operis*.

The servant or workman was bound—(1) to do Duties of Workman the work properly in the manner agreed upon; (2) he must take good care of the things entrusted to him, and was bound to pay their value if they were lost or injured through his negligence or unskilfulness. The employer, on the other hand, was bound to pay the wages agreed upon.

JETTISON (*Lex Rhodia de Jactu*).—An interest- Jettison. ing case of hire was that of a carrier of goods in ships. The customs, known as the maritime law of Rhodes, were accepted as law by the Romans when they did not conflict with special legislation. Jettison was where, in order to save a ship, a portion of the cargo was thrown overboard. The loss was divided between the owners of the goods lost and the owners of the vessel and of the cargo saved. The owner of the vessel was also entitled

to contribution when a mast was cut to save the
vessel, but not for repairs of damage done in a
storm in the course of the voyage, although the repairs were necessary to enable the vessel to continue
the voyage. The owners of the goods lost had no
direct action against the owners of the goods
saved; but they could sue the shipowner on the
contract of hire for the purpose of requiring him
to keep the goods until the contribution was paid;
or, if these had been delivered, to allow them to sue
the owners of the goods in the shipowner's name.

Sect. VII.—Partnership (*Societas*).

Partner-
ship de-
fined.

Partnership (*societas*) is a contract in which two
or more persons combine their property, or one
contributes property and another labour, with the
object of sharing amongst themselves the gains.
There cannot be a partnership in which one partner
contributes nothing—neither property nor labour.
A partner might share in the profit and not in the
loss, but a partner could not share in the loss only
and not in the profit. Such a partnership (*Leonina
Societas*) could be made only from a charitable
motive; and it was necessary in this contract that
there should be a valuable consideration moving
from each of the partners.

Roman
and
Modern
Law.

A profound difference is to be remarked between
partnership in the Roman Law and partnership

in modern systems of law. The most important *Partners not implied Agents.* aspect of partnership is the relation between the partnership and third parties who enter into transactions with any of the partners. Every partner within the scope of the business is an implied agent of the other partners, and can bind the' assets of the partnership. In Rome this was wholly wanting. (The Roman Law of partnership deals only with the claims of partners as between themselves.) The *actio pro socio* has no wider scope; and (third parties had no direct remedy except against the individual partner with whom they contracted.)

Partnership was formed by the consent of the *Shares of Partners.* parties. If nothing was said as to the shares of the partners, they took equal shares. If the share is expressed in one case only, whether of profit or loss, but omitted in the other, then in the other case that has been passed over the same share must be kept to. By express agreement, however, the share of loss might be different. Thus one partner might have two-thirds of the profit and one-third of the loss, and the other partner one-third of the profit and two-thirds of the loss. As in the case of Sale and Hire, the determination of the shares might be left to a *Dissolution of Partnership.* third party.

Partnership was ended — (1.) By renunciation.

Any partner might dissolve the partnership if no
time was fixed for its duration, and if he did not act
with a view to appropriate to himself what would
otherwise have fallen into the partnership estate.
A partner who withdrew without justification
divested himself of all his rights as a partner, but
remained liable for all obligations (*socium a se, non
se a socio liberat*). (2.) By the death of a partner,
because, in entering into a contract of partnership,
a man chooses for himself determinate persons as
his associates.   Even if the partnership was formed
by more than two persons, the death of one dissolved it although several survived, unless it was
otherwise agreed when they joined in partnership. (3.) By the loss of liberty or citizenship by
any partner.   (4.) The bankruptcy of one of the
partners, or the confiscation of all his property,
dissolved the partnership.   But in this case, if the
members agree to go on as partners, a new partnership is begun.   (5.) A partnership is at an end
when it was formed for some special business, and
that business is finished.   Again, a partnership is
terminated—(6.) By the loss of the partnership
property; (7.) By the lapse of time for which
it was formed; and (8.) By one of the partners
commencing an action to enforce his rights.

Kinds of
Partner-
ship.

Five kinds of partnership were distinguished—

(1.) Trade Partnership (*Societas universorum quae*

ex quaestu veniunt); such as that of bankers or money-lenders. This was the partnership understood to be made, if no other form was specially agreed upon. The partners contribute definite property, and they divide the profits arising from it according to their shares.

(2.) Partnership for a single transaction (*Societas negotiationis alicujus*), as when one person contributes three horses to a team and another one, in order by selling them together to realise a higher price.

(3.) *Societas vectigalium*, or a partnership between persons farming out the taxes.

(4.) *Societas unius rei*, or joint-ownership, is not a contract, but was considered under that category, because where joint-ownership had originated by agreement between two persons, they could employ the *actio pro socio* for an account as between them.

(5.) *Societas universorum bonorum* resembles the Hindoo institution of the joint family. It means that two persons agree to have a common purse. All that they acquire, from whatever source, becomes joint-property, and they are entitled to have all their debts and expenses paid out of the common fund.

The reciprocal rights and duties of partners were few and simple. 1. Each must contribute what has been agreed upon, and whatever he gains

Duties of Partners.

in respect of partnership transactions. 2. Each is entitled to be reimbursed all expenses properly incurred, and to be indemnified in respect of all the obligations he undertakes on behalf of the partnership. 3. Each partner was liable for wilful default (*dolus*), but not for negligence in the ordi-

Culpa. nary sense. It was enough that a partner displayed such diligence and care in regard to the partnership concerns as he usually did in regard to his own. This was decided on a ground that would equally apply to all contracts whatever—that a man who takes to himself a partner lacking in diligence has nobody to complain of but himself.

SECT. VIII.—EXTINCTION OF CONTRACTS : NOVATION.

Contracts were extinguished (1) by actual performance (*solutio*) or its equivalents; (2) by release; (3) by prescription; (4) by suit (*litis contestatio*) ; and (5) by merger (*confusio*).

Perfor-   1. *Solutio.*—Every obligation may be discharged
mance. by the giving of what is due, or, if the creditor consents, of something else in its place. It matters not who discharges it, whether the debtor or someone else for him ; for he is freed even if someone else discharges it, and that whether the debtor knew it or not, and even if it was done against his will. If, without the fault of the promisor, it becomes impossible to fulfil the promise, generally

the promisor was discharged. A. promises by
stipulation to give a small plot of land to another.
Before doing so, the owner of the ground buries a
dead body in it, and so makes it *religiosa* and
extra commercium. A. cannot be compelled to
pay damages for non-performance.

2. Release is of two kinds—formal and non- Formal
formal. The Roman Law started with the idea
that no debtor could be released, except by a
proceeding analogous to that by which he bound
himself. (*Nihil tam naturale est quam eo genere
quidque dissolvere quo colligatum est.*—D. 50, 17,
35.) Hence a contract of *nexum* made by *mancipatio* must be dissolved by *mancipatio ;* a contract
by stipulation must be dissolved by stipulation
(*acceptilatio*) ; a contract formed by writing (*expen-
sum ferre*), by written release (*acceptum ferre*).
This rule, founded on a false analogy, was inconvenient, and an ingenious device was introduced by
Gallus Aquilius, a colleague of Cicero. If by an Aquilian
existing contract a person was bound to do or give tion.
anything, and he afterwards by stipulation promised to do or to give the same thing, then the
original contract was considered at an end, and its
place taken by the stipulation, upon which alone
henceforth the promisor could be sued. Taking
advantage of this peculiarity, Aquilius introduced
a general form embracing every kind of obligation,

and converted all these obligations into a single stipulation. Then, by another stipulation, the creditor released this obligation, and thus all the obligations of one person to another could be discharged at a single stroke.

Non-formal Release.

By a formal release, the legal tie (*vinculum juris*) was broken. If there were sureties, they were *ipso facto* released; if the release was made to one of several co-debtors, all were immediately free. At first the Roman Law recognised no release from a formal contract except a formal release. [But at length the Praetor interfered to protect a debtor whom his creditor had agreed to acquit, but without observing the appropriate formalities. If a creditor agreed not to sue, it was against good conscience afterwards to allow him to molest the debtor.

Pact not to sue.

The Praetor gave effect to such an agreement (*pactum de non petendo*) by refusing to the creditor his legal remedy. This was not quite the same thing as a release. A formal release wholly extinguished the obligation for every purpose; an agreement not to sue might operate in favour of some of the parties and not of others; it might be subject to conditions; everything depended on the terms of the agreement. Thus in the case of a suretyship, a release by *acceptilatio* of either principal or surety put an end to the suretyship; but an agreement made with

a surety did not create even a presumption in
favour of the release of the principal, although an
agreement not to sue the principal was *prima facie*
an acquittance of the surety. The reason was that
if the surety were called on to pay, he would have
his indemnity from the principal, who would thus
in the end derive no benefit from his acquittance.

3. *Statutes of Limitation.*—No general statute Prescrip-
of limitations for obligations was introduced until tion.
far down in the Empire, by Theodosius, in A.D.
424. Actions derived from the *jus civile* were perpetual, and so strong was the idea of an obligation
as a chain (*vinculum*) that the Romans had some
difficulty in conceiving the possibility of its being
unloosed except by the proper legal key. No such
difficulty affected the Praetor. When he interfered in derogation of the civil law, his action was
always regarded as an extraordinary stretch of
power, fully justified and required by natural
justice, but still anomalous. Penal actions created
by the Praetor must be brought within one year;
but actions brought in for the recovery of property
were perpetual. In the latter, as in most other
cases, the statutory period of limitation in the time
of Justinian was thirty years.

4. When an action was commenced and had
gone so far as to be referred to an *arbiter* or *judex*
(*litis contestatio*), the obligation was gone.

I

5. Before the change in the law introduced by
Justinian, if an heir was either debtor or creditor
to the person whom he succeeded, then as the
heir and the deceased were in law regarded as one
person, the debt was extinguished (*confusio*).

Novation defined.   NOVATION.—In its most general sense *novatio*
means any change in the form or in the parties to an
obligation.   Thus if A. owes 10 *aurei* to B., we may
have three principal changes.   B. may transfer his
right to C.   A. will then be debtor to C.

Or B. may accept D. as his debtor in place of A.
D. will then owe the 10 *aurei* to B.

Or, while A. and B. remain the same, the simple
debt of 10 *aurei*, arising, for example, from a sale
or loan, may be changed into a sum due by stipulation.

Transfer of Claims.   A creditor could, without the consent of the
debtor, transfer his right to a third party. Upon
giving notice to the debtor, the new creditor could
in his own name bring an action for the debt, subject to the right of the debtor to set up against him
whatever defence he had against the original creditor.   To prevent debtors being too much harassed,
the law, in the time of Justinian, was that a transferee of a claim could not receive more than he paid
for it with interest.

Delegation.   When, by the consent of the creditor, a new debtor was substituted for the old, *delegatio* was said to take place. It was done by the creditor stipulating with the new debtor for the debt, by which means the old obligation was taken away. Justinian made a very important change in the law on this point. The principle of the Roman Law was, that whether a new stipulation for the same object as an existing obligation took away that obligation or not, depended entirely upon the intention of the parties. But a number of presumptions were introduced as to the circumstances in which such an intention was to be inferred. Justinian removed all doubts by enacting that there should be no novation, unless it was expressly declared by the contracting parties that such was the aim of their agreement. If not, both the original and the new obligation remained in force. *(margin: Change by Justinian.)*

Again, while the parties to a contract remained the same, the form of their contract might be altered. The common case was the merger of an obligation by making a *stipulatio*. The enactment of Justinian just stated applied to this case as well as to *delegatio*. *(margin: Merger.)*

SECT. IX.—SURETYSHIP.

When one person undertook to answer for the debt or obligation of another, whether as his *(margin: Contracts of Suretyship.)*

substitute by novation (*expromissor*), or in addition
to him (*adpromissor*), he was said to be an *inter-
cessor.* The contract of suretyship could be made
by stipulation (in three forms), by mandate, and
by the *pactum de constituto.* Earliest in point of
time are the forms of suretyship by stipulation.

Sponsio. The oldest of all (*Sponsio*) could be made only
by Roman citizens, and only as ancillary to a debt
Fidepro- created by stipulation. *Fidepromissio* (so called
missio. from the words used, *Fidepromittis? Fidepromitto*)
was likewise ancillary to stipulations, but it could
be made by aliens as well as by citizens. Both
forms were obsolete in the time of Justinian, and
Fidejussio. they had been long replaced by *fidejussio* (from the
words *Fidejubes? Fidejubeo*), which could be annexed
not merely to stipulations but to every species of
Mandate. obligation, whether natural or civil. By mandate
also, without *stipulatio*, a suretyship could be constituted. Thus, if Titius, at the request of Gaius,
lent money to Maevius, an obligation upon Gaius
was implied to make good the amount if Maevius
failed to repay it. Thus Gaius was a surety.
Necessarily, however, such a liability could arise
only in respect of future debts, incurred by the
creditor on the faith of the mandate. If the debt
actually existed, and the creditor pressed for pay-
Pactum ment, anyone who promised to see the debt paid,
de Con-
stituto. in consideration of the creditor forbearing to sue,

became a surety. Such an agreement was called a *pactum de constituto.*

Women were prohibited by the *Senatus Con-* Women not Sure-
sultum Velleianum (temp. Vespasian, probably) ties.
from undertaking to answer for the debt of others, whether as sureties or as substitutes (*ex-promissores*). Custom refused to women not only offices of state, but business duties, which imply their going into the company of men away from their own homes. They were therefore prohibited from undertaking gratuitous responsibilities, and exposing their property to danger. The terms of the enactment were sweeping. It forbade every woman to make any contract or give any of her property as security on behalf of any person (even a husband, son, or father) to any creditor. An *intercessio* by a woman was wholly void.

According to the law as it stood in the time Debtor to
of Justinian, the surety could not be sued until be sued
the principal debtor had made default (*beneficium* before
ordinis), except in the case of bankers, who had Surety.
the option of suing the surety first. If the principal debtor was beyond the jurisdiction, and could not be sued, the surety was allowed a reasonable time to bring him into court, and, if he failed, could himself be sued in the first instance. The creditor, if he compelled the surety to pay, must surrender to him every mortgage or pledge that he had in

respect of the debt. In the event of the surety
being required to pay, he was entitled to sue the
principal debtor to repay him the amount. His
remedy was the *actio mandati.*

CO-SURETIES.—Before the time of the Emperor
Hadrian there existed no kind of right to contribution between co-sureties, where one only had been
sued and compelled to pay the whole debt. A
surety when sued could object to pay unless the
creditor first transferred to him his right of action
against the other sureties (*beneficium cedendarum
actionum*). But Hadrian introduced a species of
contribution (*beneficium divisionis*). The surety who
was sued could require the creditor to divide his
claim among the sureties that were solvent at the
time issue was joined in the action. If any of the
sureties were insolvent, the burden upon the rest
was increased. But if the surety neglected to claim
the privilege of division, and the creditor obtained
the whole amount from him, there was no right
of contribution against the co-sureties.

Contribu-
tion be-
tween Co-
Sureties.

SECT. X.—QUASI-CONTRACT.

English lawyers distinguish between express and
implied contracts. Under the name of implied
contracts are included many true contracts, when
the consent of the parties has not been expressed

Implied
Contracts.

but may be reasonably inferred ; but other obligations are included that are not based on the consent of the parties, and are not contracts at all.
The term (quasi-contract) might conveniently be
borrowed from the Roman Law as a name for
those obligations, or rights *in personam*, that are
not derived from the consent of the parties, but
are imposed by law regardless of their assent or
dissent.) The chief examples in the Roman Law
are the *Condictio Indebiti* to recover money paid
by mistake, and the *actio negotiorum gestorum.*

Money paid under a mistake of fact could be **Money paid by Mistake.**
recovered, but as a rule not money paid under a
mistake of law. If the money were a debt of
honour (*naturalis obligatio*) and voluntarily paid,
it could not be demanded back. Money paid by
order of a court is not money paid by mistake,
even when the order is wrong. So money paid
to avoid the risk of a penalty is not considered
as paid by mistake. The general rule was that
a person was to suffer from ignorance of law, **Ignorance of Law and Fact.**
but not from ignorance of fact. The reason
assigned was, that the law is, or ought to be,
knowable ; but the most prudent man cannot
know everything. The ground upon which the
Roman jurists placed the distinction seems to
rest upon the idea of negligence, so that a man
could not plead ignorance of a fact that was well

known to everybody but himself. Minors under twenty-five, women, soldiers, peasants, and some others were not made responsible even for ignorance of law.

Negotiorum gestio. The *Negotiorum gestio* is to be compared with mandate. To act on behalf of another at his request was mandate; to act for him without his knowledge or request was *negotiorum gestio.* This was introduced for public convenience, lest when men were forced to hurry away suddenly, and went from home without giving any one a mandate to look after their affairs, their business should be neglected. No one, under such circumstances, would attend to the interests of the absent if they had no action to recover what they spent. The *negotiorum gestor,* although he acted gratuitously, yet interfered voluntarily, and was bound to act with the care of a good *paterfamilias;* it was not enough to use the diligence he ordinarily displayed in his own affairs.

SECT. XI.—DELICTS.

Division of Delicts. Delicts or wrongs may be against the person or against property. In the Roman Law this distinction is very emphatic. A wrong to the person was an *injuria;* harm done to property was *damnum injuria.*

Injuria, *Injuria* is when a person, either intentionally or

by negligence, violates any right that a free man
has in respect of his own person. It thus includes
a multifarious variety of wrongs, as striking or
whipping a man ; kidnapping or falsely imprisoning
him ; reviling a man in public (*convicium facere*) ;
defaming a man either by words or writing, or
even by acts. Thus it was defamation to take
possession of a man's goods, as if he were insolvent, when he owed nothing. Again, it was an
injuria to enter a man's house against his will,
even to serve a summons. Attempts directed
against chastity, and the administration of love-
philtres, were *injuriae*.

An assault was not an *injuria* if committed in Self-
self-defence. When one's life or limb was threat-
Defence
ened, any amount of force to repel the injury was
lawful, if it was reasonably necessary. A man put
in fear of his life could, with impunity, kill his
assailant ; but if he could have caught the man,
and there was no necessity for killing him, he was
not justified. In defence of property less latitude
was allowed. Even a burglar could not be lawfully
killed, if the householder could spare his life without peril to himself. Any less violence was,
however, justifiable in defence of property.

An *injuria* was held to be aggravated (*atrox*) by Aggra-
considerations—(1) of the nature of the act, as Injury.
vated
when a man is wounded, or scourged, or beaten

with sticks ; (2) of the place, as when the assault is in a public assembly ; (3) of the person, as when parents are struck by children, or patrons by freedmen ; (4) or of the part wounded, as a blow in the eye. In these cases exemplary damages were given.

Slaves and Injuria. There could be no *injuria* to a slave. A slave was susceptible of damage, of depreciation as a money-making machine (*damnum injuria*), but not of *injuria.* In two ways, however, a more humane doctrine was established. First, it was held that whipping a slave was a constructive insult to the master, whose exclusive privilege it was to flog his own slave ; and thus, although the slave was not injured, the master could sue for the insult to himself. Again, when the injury was severe, the Praetor granted an action to the master, even when from the circumstances there could have been no intention to insult the master. In the case of persons under **Filii-familias.** *potestas*, the rule was that they could suffer *injuria* ; but only their *paterfamilias* could, except in certain rare cases, sue for the injury. The *paterfamilias* sued both on his own account and his son's, and was entitled to damages on both grounds. In like **Wives.** manner, a husband sued for *injuria* done to his wife.

Division of Wrongs to Property. Wrongs to property are to be distinguished in the Roman Law in the case of moveables and immoveables by the nature of the respective remedies. A right to a moveable may be violated in several ways; first, by depriving the owner of possession, and that either by stealth (*furtum*) or by violence (*vi bonorum raptorum*); and, secondly, without depriving the owner of possession by damaging his property, and impairing its usefulness (*damnum injuria*). -

Theft is defined in the Institutes of Justinian to be the dealing with an object, or with its use or possession, with intent to defraud. To deal with the use or possession of a thing in a manner forbidden by the owner was theft. Thus if a creditor, who is entitled merely to the possession of the thing pledged, used it ; or if a person with whom a thing was deposited for custody only, used it ; or if a person borrowed a thing for one purpose and used it for another—in all those cases the parties were guilty of stealing the use (*furtum usus*). If an owner who had pledged a thing secretly carried it off from the creditor, or an owner finding his own lost property in the lawful possession of another, surreptitiously took it away, the owner was said to steal the possession of the thing (*furtum possessionis*). When a person attempted to seduce a slave to steal his master's property, and, in order to catch the tempter the master allowed the slave to carry some goods to him, the old jurists were in

Theft : its Kinds.

great perplexity, because the owner seemed to have consented to the removal. Justinian brushed aside the difficulty, and declared that not only the action for theft, but the action for corrupting a slave (*actio servi corrupti*) should be brought against the tempter.

Theft from Persons interested. An action for theft could be brought not merely by owners, but by any one who, in consequence of being responsible for the loss of anything, was interested in its safe custody. Every person who was under a legal obligation to take care of any property was considered in fault if the thing was stolen. Thus, if a fuller or tailor takes clothes to be cleaned and done up or to be mended for a fixed price, and **Hirers.** they are stolen from him, it is he, and not the owner, that can bring the action for theft. The owner had no interest, as he could sue the fuller or tailor for the value of the things stolen. But if the fuller or tailor were insolvent, the owner was allowed to sue the thief. A similar rule prevailed **Borrowers.** in the case of gratuitous loan (*commodatum*) till Justinian altered the law. Justinian gave the owner an option of proceeding either against the borrower or against the thief. If the owner knew that the thing was stolen, and commenced an action against one, he was not allowed to stop that action and sue the other. He had made his election. If, however, he began an action against the

borrower in ignorance of the theft, he was allowed
to give up his claim against the borrower and to
proceed against the thief. If the thief were solvent,
there was an advantage in suing him, as he was
liable to a penalty of double the value of the thing
stolen. In the case of a gratuitous deposit, the Depositees
person with whom the thing was deposited was not
answerable for negligence, and therefore not for
loss by theft. Accordingly in this case the owner,
and not the depositee, had the action against the
thief.

In the Roman Law, theft was treated as a mere Criminal
Thefts.
civil wrong subjecting the culprit to an action for
penalties ; but not even in the latest times, except
in a few aggravated cases, to punishment as a
criminal. Cattle-stealing, burglary, housebreaking,
stealing from public baths, or from a house on
fire, were punished criminally ; but in other cases,
the thief was exposed merely to a civil action. The Civil
Penalties.
penalties varied according to an ancient and curious
rule. If the thief was caught in the act (*furtum
manifestum*) the penalty was fourfold the value of
the thing stolen ; if he were not (*furtum nec manifestum*), the penalty was twofold (besides restitu-
tion of the stolen property). Many subtle questions ✓
were raised upon this distinction. Justinian decided
that it was "manifest theft" so long as the thief was
seen or taken in possession of the stolen goods by

any one, before he reached the place where he meant to carry them and lay them down.

Robbery. [In the case of robbery (*actio vi bonorum raptorum*) the penalty was fourfold if the action was brought within a year; after a year, only for the value. The fourfold penalty included the recovery of the thing taken.] The rules relating to robbery are but a repetition of the rules applicable to theft. But at this point Justinian notices the distinction between robbery and the violent seizure of goods under a claim of right. By statute, it was established that [if an owner forcibly reclaimed his property, he should forfeit it to the person from whom he took it \ if a person, not owner, but thinking himself owner, did so, he was bound to restore the property, and then pay its value.

Claim of Right.

Damnum injuria. The law relating to damage to property (*damnum injuria*) rests on the provisions of a plebiscite, known as the *lex Aquilia*, carried by Aquilius, a tribune of the plebs, in B.C. 286. This law abrogated and superseded the provisions of the earlier law, including the XII Tables. It was not a scientific enactment; it distinguished only two classes of injuries, each characterised by a distinct and arbitrary measure of damages. [The first class was the killing of a slave or four-footed beast reckoned among cattle. The penalty was the highest value that the property bore within the year preceding.

All other damage to slaves, animals, moveables or
even immoveables, was included in the second category, and the measure of damages was the highest
value within the thirty days preceding the injury.
If the defendant denied his liability, and was condemned, he had to pay double damages. The
enactment, as it was drawn, made no provision
for indirect injuries. Thus to throw a stone at a
horse and hurt him entailed liability ; but to lay
down a stone and trip a horse was not visited
with damages. This defect was remedied by the
Praetor. The statute gave an action only when Direct and
the damage was done to a body by a body (*corpore* Indirect Damages.
corpori); but the Praetor after the analogy of the
statute gave a remedy when the damage was done
not directly by the body (*non corpore sed corpori*),
and even when no damage was done to the thing
itself (*nec corpore nec corpori*). In the first case, the
action was said to be *utilis* in the second case,
an actio in factum, as it was called, was granted.
Thus if I shut up another man's slave or cattle,
and starve them to death, or drive a beast so
furiously as to founder it, or terrify cattle to rush
over a cliff, or persuade another's slave to climb a
tree or go down a well, and he in climbing or
going down is either killed or injured in some
part of his body, then against me an *actio utilis*
is given. If, on the other hand, a man thrusts

another's slave from a bridge into a river, and the slave is drowned, then he is directly liable within the words of the statute, as it is with his body he did the damage. If, again, a man moved by pity frees another's slave from his fetters to release him, he hurts the master, but not the body of the slave; and in this case provision was made by the *actio in factum.*

Negligence. To support an action under the *lex Aquilia*, it was essential, however, that there should be not merely harm (*damnum*), but wrong (*injuria*). The damage, to be actionable, must be done either intentionally or by negligence. What constituted negligence depended upon circumstances. Two cases are cited in the Institutes. A man playing with javelins kills a slave passing by. Is he liable? If he was a soldier practising in the Campus Martius, or in any other place set apart for soldiers' practice, that did not imply negligence; but if any one else, or a soldier elsewhere, did so, the striking would *prima facie* amount to negligence. Again, if a pruner, by breaking down a branch from a tree, kills your slave as he passes, near a public road or path used by neighbours, and he did not first shout and warn the slave, he was guilty of negligence. If, on the other hand, the place was quite off the road, or in the middle of a field, he was not liable for negligence, even if he did not shout. Want of skill was considered equivalent _{Want of Skill.} to negligence for the purpose of the *lex Aquilia;* as, for instance, when a doctor kills a slave by bad surgery or by giving him wrong drugs. So if a rider or a muleteer runs over a slave he is chargeable with negligence if the damage resulted from want of skill, or even from want of the strength of an ordinary man.

In estimating the compensation due to the _{Measure of Damages.} owner, usage authorised the judges in going beyond the actual value of the slave or thing destroyed, and taking account of the loss accruing to the owner. If one of a pair of mules or team of horses was killed, or one slave out of a band of comedians or singers, the reckoning includes not merely the animal or person killed, but in addition the depreciation in value of the rest. So, if a slave who is killed has been appointed heir to a man whose estate is worth 1000 *aurei*, and by his death the inheritance is lost to his master, then the damages include, in addition to the value of the slave, 1000 *aurei*.

Immoveables, in regard to wrongs, are in a _{Torts to Land.} different position from moveables. Immoveables cannot be stolen; and if a possessor is wrongfully ejected, the law can actually restore his property, and not merely give him an equivalent in damages. In the Roman Law, the remedy for wrongful

K

ejectment was not technically called an action, but an interdict (*Interdictum de vi et vi armata*). Every injurious act done to an immoveable with-

Clam, vi.   out the consent (*clam*) or against the will (*vi*) of the owner, exposed the offending party to the interdict <u>*Quod vi aut clam*</u>, by which he was compelled to pay the expenses of undoing the mischief.

Quasi-Delict.

QUASI-DELICTS.—The wrongs above enum-erated alone were called delicts ; other wrongs were said to arise *quasi ex delicto*. In this case the prefix *quasi* indicates merely that the wrongs so described did not attract the attention of the law until a comparatively late period, when the denotation of '*delictum*' was fixed by usage. Between a delict, therefore, and a quasi-delict there was no real distinction. The quasi-delicts mentioned in the Institutes may be briefly noticed.

Wrong Judgment.   If a *judex* gave a corrupt decision, or gave a decision beyond the terms of the reference, he was liable to an action for damages at the suit of the injured party.

Suspensa.   Persons who kept anything so placed or hung that it might, if it fell, do harm to a person passing by, were subject to a penalty of 10 *aurei*, even if no one was hurt.

The occupier of a house was liable for damages *De Effuris et Dejectis.* done to any one by anything thrown out or poured down from the house, although the mischief was done not by the occupier himself, but by some one else.

A master of a ship was liable for any loss by *Edict Nautae, Cauponae, etc.* theft or damage to any goods in the ship through the misconduct of the sailors employed in the ship. The same responsibility attached to innkeepers and livery stable-keepers for goods left in the inn or in the stables.

CHAPTER V.

THE LAW OF INHERITANCE AND LEGACY.

SECT. I.—TESTAMENTARY SUCCESSION.

THE subject we now approach may be regarded as at once the most interesting and the most tedious branch of Roman Law. In its broader aspects, it supplies a fascinating chapter in the history of thought; to enter into all the detail that we find even in the Institutes would not be very instructive, and would certainly be dull. The great central fact is that the idea of a testamentary disposition of property, which, but for the plain teaching of history, we should consider of the very essence of ownership, was reached by slow and tortuous steps.

Contrast of Ancient and Modern Will. Sir Henry S. Maine has drawn attention to the sharp contrast that exists between a modern will and the instrument from which it is historically derived. A will is a secret document; it is revocable during life, until the termination of which it has no effect. The old will of the Roman Law was a conveyance *inter vivos;* it consequently took effect at once, was irrevocable, and was made openly in the presence of a number of witnesses. But that is not all. The purpose of a modern will is to divide property; the testator stands face to face with the legatees; an executor is appointed merely for convenience in winding up the estate. The primary purpose of a Roman will (even in the time of Justinian) was to appoint an executor—in other words, a universal successor to the deceased; if it failed in that, it was wholly worthless. From the legal standpoint, the nomination of the executor was the whole object of the will. That which in the real purpose of the testator was the first and paramount object—the distribution of his property —was in the eyes of the law a secondary and quite subsidiary point. Nothing can be more puzzling to a student of law than the wholly inverted manner in which, according to modern ideas, even the most recent productions of the Roman intellect deal with the subject of wills and legacies. To understand how this came about, is to master nearly everything that is of interest in this department of Roman Law.

The earliest notions of succession to deceased Hindoo persons are connected with duties rather than with Heir. rights, with sacrifices rather than with property. In the Hindoo Law, the heir or successor is the person bound to offer the funeral rites required for the comfort of the deceased's soul; and even in the Roman Law there are not wanting indications of the same fact. The property of the deceased was the natural fund to provide the expenses, in some systems of religion by no means inconsiderable, of the necessary religious ceremonies. In the Roman Law, until the change, presently to be stated, made by Justinian, the heir was considered to stand in relation to third parties as more than a representative of the deceased, as actually continuing his legal personality. The heir succeeded to all the rights and liabilities (*in universum jus*) of the deceased; and just as a person is not excused from paying his debts because he has insufficient means, so it was no answer to a creditor when suing an heir for money due by the deceased that the deceased had not left him funds wherewith to discharge his debts. Up to the alteration of the law by Justinian, *the heir was bound to pay all the debts of the deceased, even if he obtained no property from him whatever.* An insolvent inheritance was thus a veritable *damnosa hereditas.*

The history, not of Rome alone, but of other nations, shows that in the earliest times the heir was the person designated by nature to perform the duties of filial piety to the deceased. The children, or failing them, the more distant kindred, were the only successors dreamt of by the men who made the institutions of the Indo-European family. But children and kin sometimes fail. To persons actuated by the ideas and feelings of a modern European, such a circumstance would not be considered as an evil of a grave order. Far otherwise was it with men who devoutly practised the worship of ancestors, who believed that the spirits of their fathers hovered around the household hearth, and required such nourishment as could be derived from the ghost of food sacrificed to them. To die childless was to leave the perturbed spirit of the father without rest or food; from the natural protector of his house he became a malignant ghoul. The records of ancient law show many traces of the absolute horror with which the fathers of our race contemplated their disconsolate state if they died without children, and by consequence without heirs.

The ingenuity of men first provided in the fiction of adoption a remedy for this emergency. He that had no child was allowed to select a son. When in the course of nature he died, this artifice provided him with an heir. It is a disputed question whether the Hindoos ever advanced nearer to a law of testamentary succession than this rude device; and it is a significant fact, that the ancient

Adoption.

forms of adoption of the Roman Law correspond point for point with the earliest forms of true testamentary succession. Accordingly, to the Roman Law we must turn for the development of this idea.

Testamentary Succession.

Testamentary succession did not make a real beginning until men accepted the idea of the direct appointment of an heir, without going through the intermediate stage of sonship. The first testamentary heir is he that succeeds, not by natural succession, but by the will of his predecessor, directly to the deceased without being first his son. This stage is exemplified by the Roman Law. During the thousand years through which we trace the evolution of Roman genius in the region of law, one grand, central idea dominates the whole law of wills. It is that the function of the Will is to name an heir. The conception of a legacy—of the gift by the deceased of a specific part of his property to a legatee—was originally no part of the will, and might almost be said to be alien to it. Indeed, the history of this portion of the law may be summed up in the statement, that the legacy gradually encroached upon, and ended by almost superseding, the idea of universal succession, upon which was based the first introduction of wills. The Legacy came into being when first the law permitted the testator to enjoin commands upon the heir as to what he would do with this or that article of property, and when the heir was compelled to execute those commands. Finally, as will appear, if we penetrate through an outer crust of forms and a somewhat tangled story of legal learning, we shall find the Roman Law reaching a point scarcely to be distinguished from the modern view, bringing the testator into direct relation with the legatee, and reducing the ancient Heir to a mere official for distributing property.

The principle of the Roman Law until the in-troduction of inventories by Justinian was that the heir, as regards third parties, stood exactly in the shoes of the deceased, and was bound to pay all his debts, even if he obtained no property from him whatever. By the provisions of the XII Tables the testator, after his debts were paid, could bequeath the whole surplus of his estate to legatees. This freedom defeated itself. No inducement was left to the heir to accept the inheritance, who accordingly, by refusing to act, nullified the testa-ment, and deprived the legatees of everything. After two ineffectual attempts to deal with this question by legislation, in the year D.C. 39, under Augustus, a statute was passed (*Lex Falcidia*) providing that in every case the heir should have one-fourth of the clear proceeds of the estate. In estimating the clear proceeds, all the debts were

Liability of Heir.

deducted, and the funeral expenses and the price of slaves ordered to be manumitted by the will.

Inventories. Justinian introduced a profounder change in this than in any other branch of law. He broke up an association of ideas riveted by the practice of more than a thousand years. The ideas of 'heir' and of 'unlimited liability' were indissolubly associated for ages. Justinian, at one bold stroke, converted the heir into a mere official, appointed by the testator for the purpose of winding up his affairs and distributing his property. The heir now differed in nothing from a modern executor, except that he was continued in the heir's right to a fourth (*Falcidia Quarta*), unless the testator expressly forbade it, and he was entitled to the property left by the testator, in so far as it was not swallowed up in legacies. This result was accomplished by a process of gentle compulsion. If the heir did not make an inventory—setting forth all the property of the deceased—he continued liable not merely for the debts of the deceased, but, in addition, he was compelled to pay all the legacies, should the assets prove insufficient. On the other hand, if the heir made a full inventory, in compliance with the terms of the law, he was released from all personal liability for the debts of the deceased, and was not bound to pay beyond the assets that came into his hands

The essence of a Roman will, as has been already *Nature of Roman Will.* stated, was the nomination of a universal successor to a deceased person; if a will failed in that point, it was wholly and absolutely worthless; if it accomplished that object, it could, but it need not, effect other purposes, such as the gift of legacies or the appointment of tutors. So fastidious was the Roman Law in keeping up this relation between the heir and the legatee, that until Justinian altered the law, a legacy occurring in the will before the appointment of the heir was void. In respect of its juridical essence and validity, a will was nothing but a lawful mode of nominating an heir. Even after the profound change introduced by Justinian, the essence of the *Testamentum* continued to be the valid and successful appointment of an heir. If none of the heirs named in the will could or would accept the inheritance, the will was void, and the legacies failed of effect. The further progress of the Roman Law was not accomplished by an extension of the *testamentum*, but by practically superseding it, through a new mode of declaring a last will by *codicilli* and *fideicommissa*, which will be explained hereafter.

A *testamentum*, as we might infer from its history, *Essentials of Roman Will.* was an extremely complex document. In order that it should operate effectually, it must comply with five sets of conditions. (1.) Certain forms must be observed ; (2.) Certain persons must either be made heirs or be formally disinherited ; (3.) To certain persons a definite portion of the testator's property must be left ; (4.) An heir must be properly instituted ; and (5.) The testator, witnesses, and heir must be severally capable by law of taking the part assigned to them. Even when a will complied with all these conditions, it might ultimately fail, owing to circumstances arising beyond the testator's control. Nay, the will might remain perfectly good, and yet if the heir named for any reason "refused" to accept, the whole fell to the ground. A few words upon each of these points will suffice.

Forms of Will.   The old will of Republican Rome was originally a conveyance *inter vivos.* The maker of the will summoned five witnesses, Roman citizens over puberty, and a balance-holder (*libripens*). He then conveyed his whole legal status to a nominal purchaser (*familiae emptor*). At first this person was the heir, upon whom after the death of the testator devolved the duty of paying the legacies. At this stage, the transaction differed in little from an ordinary conveyance. The next step was to employ a *familiae emptor* merely for form's sake, the name of the heir being contained in a written document which was not opened till the testator's death. Up to this point, the development of the

will was carried on by the jurisconsults. The next
step was taken by the Praetor. He set forth in his
edict that when a written will was sealed with the
seals of seven witnesses (a number made up by
adding the *libripens* and *familiae emptor* to the
number of witnesses required for a *mancipatio*), he
would give the person named as heir in the will
the possession of the inheritance, even although no
formal sale took place. By subsequent imperial
legislation the signatures of the testator and witnesses were required. The written will, as it existed in the time of Justinian, had thus a threefold
origin (*jus tripertitum*). The making of the will
(*uno contextu*), and the presence of the witnesses all
together at the ceremony, were a reminiscence of
the will by *mancipatio*. The seals and number
of the witnesses came from the Praetor's edict. —
The signatures of the testator and witnesses at the
foot of the will form the contribution of imperial
legislation.

The next condition of a valid will was that if Disheri-
certain persons were not named heirs they should son. *(h.)*
be expressly disinherited. ⌊At first this applied
only to such persons as were under the *potestas* of
the deceased, and became independent (*sui juris*)
by his death. These heirs were called *sui heredes*.⌋
In the time of Justinian the law stood thus. ⌊On
pain of invalidating his will, a testator must

appoint heirs, or disinherit by name not merely *sui heredes* but all his descendants through males, whether born at the testator's death or then in the womb. Inasmuch as the testator was perfectly free to disinherit all his children, it might have been assumed that if he did not name them as heirs, he intended to exclude them from the inheritance. The true reason for this technical rule, so eminently calculated to be fatal to wills, was that the old theory of the family implied a species of copartnership in the family estate. The children became owners on the death of the *paterfamilias*, who, during his life, was the sole administrator, and the law regarded them as being owners unless something had been done to turn them out. The father had the power to do so, but unless he exercised that power, there was no vacancy to which he could nominate strangers as heirs. This conception of a family copartnership must have had its roots deep in the Roman mind before it could have maintained so long an arbitrary rule, which even the all-devouring zeal of Justinian did not remove.

Joint-Family.

Legitim. When the testamentary power was conclusively sanctioned in the XII Tables, it was recognised as in its nature exceptional, and as an invasion of the rights of the family; but no hard and fast line was adopted to prevent the testator from leaving his children destitute. A remedy, however, was introduced on the plea that the testator's will was contrary to his duty (*testamentum inofficiosum*), and that consequently he was not of sound mind when he drew up the will. The meaning was not that the father was really mad, but rather that his will ought to be treated as if he were mad. In considering this limitation of a testator's freedom, and the necessity of making some provision (*legitima portio*) for his nearest relatives, we must not forget that the children of the Roman *paterfamilias* had no rights of property, and that what they acquired in virtue of their own exertions or of the liberality of others was the property of their father. Thus to disable them, and at the same time to permit the father to give what was in morals although not in law their own property to strangers, would have been to sanction a species of injustice which it is not in the power of any father in modern times to commit. After some fluctuation, the doctrine of the Roman Law came to be that the testator should leave a fourth of the amount that would have fallen in case of intestacy to his children. Children were required in the same way to remember their parents in their wills, and even brothers and sisters were forbidden to exclude brothers and sisters in favour of strangers of doubtful reputation.

Institution of Heir.

The next point requiring the attention of a testator was the formal nomination of an heir. In early times, stated language was employed, as *Lucius Titius mihi heres esto*, but at length it was sufficient if the testator's intention was shown. The appointment must, however, be in express language ; it could not be inferred from the testator's throwing upon a person duties appropriate to an heir. ⌊In case the person first named might die

Substitution.

or decline to act, it was usual to add another to take in such an event. This was called substitution, and could be carried to any extent, usually ending with the name of a slave of the testator, who obtained his freedom, but could not refuse the inheritance.⌋ This substitution (*substitutio vulgaris*) took effect only if the person instituted heir declined ; if he once accepted, the substitution was at an end. In one case, however, the Roman Law permitted a substitute to come in even after a person instituted had accepted. A testator might say, ' Let Titius my son be my heir. If my son shall not be my heir, or if he shall become my heir, and die before he comes to puberty, then let Seius be my heir.' ⌊A son could make a will after puberty, but not before, so that in effect such a substitution (*substitutio pupillaris*) was an appointment of an heir to the son until he arrived at the age when he could name one for himself.⌋ Justinian extended this indulgence to parents of insane children to name substitute heirs until their death or the recovery of their reason. This was called *substitutio exemplaris.*

The grounds of incapacity to make a will or to be a witness or heir are not of sufficient interest to require detailed statement. They are collected in 'Roman Law,' pp. 615-624. *Incapacity.*

If a will did not comply with the proper forms, or did not name an heir, or the testator, heir, or any of the witnesses were incapable of acting their several parts, or if the testator did not expressly disinherit his children, the will was said to be *injustum, or non jure factum, or nullius momenti.* If it was right in those points, but did not make provision for the legitim (*legitima portio*) of children, it was *inofficiosum.* If the will was originally good, but no one took as heir under the will, or the testator lost his capacity before his death, it was said to be *irritum* or *destitutum.* If the testator made a new will, or his will became invalidated by the subsequent birth of a person requiring to be disinherited, the original will was *ruptum.* *Defects in Wills.*

From this brief sketch, it may be understood how perilous was the act of testation, even in the latest times. We may well ask why a people with the practical genius of the Romans for law continued to submit to a form of will that must con- *Nonformal Will.*

L

stantly have frustrated the intentions of testators
and the expectations of legatees. The explanation
of this puzzle is found in the fact that, in the time
of Augustus, a new mode of testation was introduced, which successfully enabled testators to avoid
the snares and pitfalls of the *testamentum.* The
mountain was too great to remove, but a way was
found of simply walking round it. The device
invented for this purpose was the non-formal will
Codicilli. of the Roman Law—*codicilli.* In their origin and
essence, *codicilli* present a complete contrast to the
testamentum. They were in the nature of requests
to persons who, independently of the *codicilli*, were
heirs, to give to others either some specific articles,
or a fraction or even the whole of the inheritance.
By *codicilli* a legal heir could not be appointed.
They were free from all formalities, although
Theodosius (A.D. 424) required the presence of five
witnesses ; but even if this testimony was wanting,
a person claiming as legatee could compel the heir
to tell upon oath what instructions he had received.
By *codicilli* no person could be disinherited, nor
did their validity depend upon providing legitim.
If there was no *testamentum, codicilli* operated by
way of trust on the heirs *ab intestato ;* but if
there was a *testamentum*, they were considered a
charge upon the testamentary heirs, and were made
to stand or fall with the will. If *codicilli* were

made before a *testamentum*, the *codicilli* were pre-
sumed to be cancelled, unless the contrary was
proved. It was usual, therefore, in a will to con-
firm *codicilli* previously made, if the testator wished —
them to be carried out.

We are informed by Justinian that the Romans Trusts.
owed the introduction of *codicilli* to the Emperor
Augustus. They became exceedingly popular on
account of their convenience when the Romans
were away from home, and soon a special judge was
appointed to take charge of trusts (*fideicommissa*).
These trusts were charges on the legal heir, whether
he were appointed by will or succeeded to an intestate. From the first, great latitude was allowed
in trusts. Thus aliens and Latins could take by
way of trust, although not under a will. Women
could take an inheritance by trust, free from the
restrictions of the *lex Voconia.* Again, by means
of trusts much greater flexibility was introduced in
the settlement of property. A testator by way of
trust could give his inheritance to A. for life, then ✓
to B. for life, and then to divide it between C., D.,
and E. Again, A. and B. might be heirs on trust
that, if one died without children, his share should
go to the survivor, and, if both died without children, the whole should go to C. Such limitations
were impossible in a *testamentum.*

In one respect *fideicommissa* were slow in attaining maturity. When a testator—to take a simple case—charged his heir to give up one-half of the inheritance to another, it was no easy task rightly to adjust the relations of the two persons. The maxim of the Roman Law was,—once an heir, always an heir. An heir could part with the goods he received, but he could not divest himself of his liabilities. The first plan was to sell the portion of the inheritance subject to the trust to the person named for a nominal sum, and require him to guarantee the heir against a corresponding amount of the debts. In A.D. 62, in the time of Nero, the *Senatus Consultum Trebellianum* was made, providing that, in the case of inheritances wholly or partially given up under a trust, the actions heretofore given to or against the heir, should be given to and against those to whom under the will the property was required to be surrendered. This statute was perfect, except in one point. It did not compel the legal heir to enter *pro forma* and transfer the inheritance. In a mature law of trusts it is an elementary maxim that a trust shall not fail from want of a trustee; but in this early stage of their growth, the maxim was that the trust must fail unless there was a trustee.

The next step was characteristic. By the *Senatus Consultum Pegasianum* (A.D. 70), a bribe was offered to the heir to enter ; he was allowed to retain a clear fourth. | This, by analogy to the Falcidian fourth, was known as the *Quarta Pegasiana.* If, then, a legal heir was left by the will a fourth, or upwards, he entered, and the *Senatus Consultum Trebellianum* divided the liabilities in proportion to the shares of the inheritance. But if less than a fourth was left by will, the heir claimed the benefit of the *Quarta Pegasiana*, and in this case the other statute did not apply, and at law the heir was saddled with the whole debts. Accordingly, in this case again, the old plan of a nominal sale of a portion of the inheritance was gone through, and mutual guarantees made by the heir and the beneficiary. Finally, Justinian put the law on a clear footing. He enacted that in every case the heir should enter, with the benefit of the *Senatus Consultum Trebellianum*, but that he should, nevertheless, have the benefit of the Pegasian fourth.—

One step alone remained to complete the development of the law of testation. |It became usual to insert in wills a clause to the effect that if for any reason the instrument failed as a will, it should be regarded as *codicilli*, and so bind the heirs *ab intestato.*| This clause (*clausula codicillaris*) healed every defect in a will ; for the beneficiaries, if they could not sue under the will,

Codicillary Clause.

could compel the heirs *ab intestato* to execute the provisions of the instrument as trusts.

SECT. II.—INTESTATE SUCCESSION.

Three Periods. The law of intestate succession is most conveniently considered in three periods. The first takes the law as it stood at the time of the XII Tables; the third deals with the law as finally settled by Justinian, after the publication of the Institutes; and the second covers the space intervening. The first and the third periods are characterised by logical rigour and simplicity; the middle period is one of confusing transition. At the time of the XII Tables the inheritance descended to the family as based on the *potestas*. A father and an emancipated son were in law absolute strangers for the purpose of succession. By Justinian's latest enactments, the *potestas* is disregarded, and relationship is based on the tie of blood. In the language of the jurists agnation is superseded by cognation. In the interval between the XII Tables and the final legislation of Justinian, we trace the successive steps by which the natural came finally to supersede the artificial tie.

Order of Succes. SUCCESSION ACCORDING TO THE XII TABLES.

The classes that took an inheritance were as

follows :—(1) *sui heredes;* (2) in default of these, *agnati;* and (3) in default of these, *gentiles.*

Sui heredes were all those persons under the *potestas* or *manus* of the deceased who became independent on his death. Hence emancipated children, and daughters, if married and in the *manus* of their husbands, could not succeed to their father. On the other hand adopted children did succeed. *Sui heredes* took equal shares, the males not taking more than the females, nor the elder more than the younger. If some were children and others descendants of children, those descendants took only the share that their parent would have taken if alive.

Agnati formed a wider group, having the same centre, but a larger circumference. Persons are *agnati* when they are so related to a common ancestor that if they had been alive together with him, they would have been under his *potestas.* The constitution of a Roman family under the *potestas* has already been considered (pp. 27, 28). The agnates nearest in kinship excluded the more remote, and those in an equal degree of propinquity took equal shares. Failing *agnati,* the members of the *gens* to which the deceased belonged took the inheritance. Who these were, is a problem too difficult to consider here.—(*See* 'Roman Law,' pp. 656-659.)

Succession from the XII Tables to Justinian.

Changes by Prae-tor. It would be wearisome and uninstructive to trace the changes from the XII Tables to Justinian in detail. But the broader features may be indicated. [The Praetor introduced two great innovations. First, he allowed emancipated children to succeed along with *sui heredes*; and he allowed more distant blood relations (*cognati*) to come in after the *agnati*. Thus according to the Praetor the order of succession was—(1) children (*unde liberi*), whether under *potestas* or not ; (2) statutory heirs (*unde legitimi*), consisting principally of *agnati*; and (3) *cognati*, or blood relations not included in the previous classes.]

Statutory Changes. Again, by the *Senatus Consultum Tertullianum* (A.D. 158), freeborn women having three children, or freedwomen having four, were enabled to succeed to their children ; and by the *Senatus Consultum Orphitianum* (A.D. 178), children were permitted to succeed to their mothers.

Justinian's Final Legislation. Novels 118 and 127.

Order of Succes-sion. Justinian regulated succession in three classes —(1) Descendants ; (2) Ascendants, along with brothers and sisters ; and (3) Collaterals.

[*First.* Descendants excluded all others. Children take equal shares ; grandchildren take the share their parent would have taken if alive.]

Secondly. Failing descendants, ascendants came in along with brothers and sisters of the whole blood. Children of a deceased sister or brother took that person's share.]

Thirdly. Failing those, the next of kin succeed, the nearer excluding the more remote, and those in the same degree taking equal shares.

VESTING OF AN INHERITANCE.—For the purpose of vesting, heirs are divisible in the Roman Law into three classes—(1) *Necessarii heredes;* (2) *Sui et necessarii heredes;* and (3) *Extranei heredes.*

A necessary heir is a slave of the deceased *Necessarius Heres.* declared free and appointed heir by his master's will. He could not refuse the inheritance.] Hence, as a last resort, a slave was named heir to prevent his master's inheritance, in case he died insolvent, from being sold in his master's name, and thereby bringing upon him posthumous ignominy.

The *sui et necessarii heredes* were those under the *Sui Heredes.* *potestas* of deceased. At first they could not, any more than slaves, decline the inheritance; and they succeeded without the necessity of any actual acceptance. [The Praetor gave them the privilege of refusal (*beneficium abstinendi*) if they did not interfere with the inheritance.)

Extranei heredes embraced all other persons. Other Heirs.

They did not become heirs until they accepted (*aditio hereditatis*), either expressly and formally, or by acts of interference with the property of deceased.

Sect. III.—Legacy.

Basis of Law of Legacy. The law of bequest was founded on a single principle, namely, the intention of the testator. The rights of the legatee, and all the incidents connected with the legacy, have no other origin than the will of the testator. The law of bequest is therefore simply the interpretation of legacies. But the will of a testator is limited by two circumstances, one permanent, the other local and temporary. Everywhere the will of a testator is circumscribed by the general laws of his country. The State defines what property can be bequeathed, who may be legatees, and subject to what restrictions testation will be allowed. But in Rome, beyond these general limits, narrower restraints were imposed by the spirit of legal Formalism that pervaded every branch of the law. It was the universal tendency of the old Roman Law to prefer the form to the spirit; and thus, in the law of legacy, the intention of the testator was not respected unless it was expressed in one or other of certain precise forms.

Old Forms of Bequest. During the Republic a legacy must be made in one of four forms. The first was said to be *per vindica-tionem,* because it transferred the ownership of the thing bequeathed to the legatee immediately that the heir entered. It ran in this form :—'To Lucius Titius I give and bequeath the slave Stichus.' The second was *per damnationem.* It imposed a duty on the heir. 'Let my heir be condemned to give Stichus, my slave, to Lucius Titius.' These were the chief forms, the others were mere variations. The third, called *sinendi modo,* ran thus, 'Let my heir be condemned to allow Lucius Titius to take and have for himself the slave Stichus.' The fourth, *per praeceptionem,* was to this effect :—'Let Lucius Titius pick out (*praecipito*) first the slave Stichus,' that is, before the division of the inheritance, Titius being here taken to be a co-heir.

The introduction of trusts (*fideicommissa*) in the time of Augustus afforded a means of escape from the narrow pedantry of the old forms of legacy. During the Empire, the two systems continued side by side. A testator might rely upon the old rules, or, if they did not suit his purpose, he could take advantage of trusts. Justinian fused the old law with the newer equity, and enacted that legacies should be construed with all the liberality of trusts, and that trusts should be enforced by all the remedies applicable to legacies. The law was

Trusts and Legacies.

Fusion of Law and Equity.

thus placed on a simple and right foundation. It rested upon the intention of the testator, and it was carried out by direct and appropriate actions.

Donatio Mortis Causa. A gift in anticipation of death (*donatio mortis causa*) was made subject to nearly all the rules of legacies. Such a gift was made to the donee, or to any one on his behalf, on condition that it should be his property if the donor died ; but that if the donor should survive the anticipated peril, he should have his property back. Such a gift required to be attested by five witnesses.

Legacy of Mortgaged Property. The law of legacy is a law of detail, and cannot well be summarised. It will be sufficient in this place to advert to a few points. When the property bequeathed was mortgaged, the heir was bound to pay off the mortgage, unless he could prove either that the testator was not aware of the mortgage, or that the testator expressly charged the legatee to pay it off. Again, money due to a

Legacy of Debts. testator might be the object of a legacy, and if it were not paid in the testator's lifetime (in which case the legacy was extinguished), the heir was bound to permit the legatee to sue the debtor in his name. If the testator bequeathed to a debtor the amount due to him, the debtor could demand a formal release from the heir. A legacy of a sum due by the testator to his creditor was inept, unless it differed in some respect from the debt.

The chief distinction in legacies was between specific and general legacies. When a testator bequeathed a determinate, specific thing, then upon the entry of the heir the legatee became owner. If a quantity of anything was bequeathed, the legatee was simply a creditor of the heir for the amount. | By a legacy of 20 *aurei*, the relation merely of debtor and creditor was established ; but a legacy of all the *aurei* in a chest made the legatee owner of the particular coins. Specific Legacies.

Error in names was harmless. So a false description did not annul a legacy (*falsa demonstrationon nocet*). When a part of the description is sufficient to identify the object or person, and the remainder of the description is unnecessary for that purpose, the falsehood of this superflous addition is immaterial. But if the whole of the description is necessary and part of it is erroneous, the legacy fails. A testator had two slaves, Philonicus, a baker, and Flaccus, a fuller. He bequeathed to his wife Flaccus the baker. If the testator knew the names of the slaves, Flaccus will be the legacy ; if he knew them by their occupations and not by their names, Philonicus will be given. On the contrary, if A. bequeaths to B. the sum Titius owes to A., and Titius owes nothing, the legacy must fail, as there is nothing to determine the legacy except the amount due by Titius. Mistake ✓
Falsa Demonstratio.

Falsa Causa. Akin to this is the rule that a mistaken inducement (*falsa causa*) does not vitiate a legacy, as when one says, 'To Titius, because in my absence he looked after my business, I give and leave Stichus,' or, 'To Titius, because by his advocacy I was cleared of a capital charge, I give and leave Stichus.' For although Titius never managed any business for the testator, and although his advocacy never cleared him, yet the legacy takes effect. But if the heir could prove that the testator would not have left the legacy but for his erroneous belief, he could defeat the legatee on the ground that his claim was against good conscience (*exceptio doli mali*).

Restraints on Alienation. Among the restraints on testation only two call here for special notice. A testator could not bequeath property and forbid the legatee to alien it ; but according to a rescript of Severus and Antoninus, although a general prohibition to alienate was void, yet if the restriction was made in the interest of a limited class, as children, freedmen, heirs, or any specified person, it was upheld, of course without prejudice to the creditors of the testator. In this way a very strict entail might be estab-

Restraints on Marriage. lished. A similar rule applied to conditions in restraint of marriage. If the legatee or heir were forbidden to marry anybody, the legacy or will was perfectly good, and the restriction was null and void. But a condition that the heir or legatee should not marry a particular person or persons was good.

A legacy might be revoked by express language, or if the thing bequeathed perished. A revocation was implied from a serious quarrel arising between the testator and the legatee after the making of the legacy. A testator gave his freedman a legacy, and in a subsequent will described him as ungrateful. This was held to be an implied revocation. A subsequent mortgage of the thing bequeathed did not revoke the legacy; on the contrary, the presumption was that the testator intended the heir to pay off the mortgage. If the testator alienated the property, the presumption was that he meant to revoke the legacy, and it was for the legatee, if he could, to prove the contrary. If, however, the alienation was prompted by necessity, the burden of proving an intention to revoke lay on the heir.

Revocation of Legacies

CHAPTER VI.

THE LAW OF PROCEDURE.

Historical Interest of Roman Procedure. THE interest attaching to the Roman Law of Procedure is mainly historical. From the pages of Gaius, we can trace, in outline at least, the steps by which civil procedure was brought to a satisfactory condition. The history of Procedure is, in one word, the history of the efforts of the State to control the transactions of men. It is the history of the growth of jurisdiction. At first the right of the State to interfere in private quarrels Jurisdiction springs from Arbitration. is not recognised; but later on, the Roman magistrate appears in the guise of a voluntary arbitrator, a character that insensibly changed into a compulsory arbitrator. For the sake of clearness, it will be convenient to illustrate this proposition by examining the history of procedure under four heads. These shall be, in order, the successive steps in a lawsuit:—(1) the summons to court; (2) proceedings from the appearance of the parties in court till judgment; (3) execution of judgments; and (4) appeals.

THE SUMMONS.—The process of summoning a Summons. defendant to court exhibits, in a marked manner, the early characteristics of civil jurisdiction. By the law of the XII Tables a complainant personally summoned a defendant. If the defendant refused, he could call witnesses to his refusal, and thereupon drag him before the court. The law did not impose a legal duty upon the defendant to obey, and if he did not go, no further proceedings could be taken; all that the XII Tables authorised was, on proof of a refusal, that the complainant might use force, without incurring any liability. The Praetor, however, carried the law a step further. He made it an offence to refuse obedience to a summons, or to rescue a person summoned, or in any way to aid his escape. Thus by the action of the Praetor, the Roman magistrate assumed a right to hear all disputes, and the first step in civil jurisdiction was estab- ⟩ lished. Later on, under the Empire, the summons was served by a public officer, and it was made in writing (*libellus conventionis*), containing a precise statement of the demands of the complainant.

FROM APPEARANCE TILL JUDGMENT.—Until Reference the reign of Diocletian (with a few exceptions not tion. requiring notice in this place) a true civil court did not exist in Rome. To those who read warm eulogies on the civil procedure of Republican Rome, this statement may appear a strange paradox. It admits, however, of a simple demonstration. Before the time of Diocletian, the ordinary civil trial in Rome consisted in a reference to arbitration. What happened was exactly the same as if in an English suit, at the close of the pleadings, a case, instead of being tried by a judge and jury, or by a judge alone, was immediately referred to one or more arbitrators selected by the parties themselves, these arbitrators being laymen, and not lawyers.

The arbitrator, if only one was chosen, was *Judex.* called *judex or arbiter*, the distinction between which Cicero in one passage seems to regard as *Arbiter.* an idle quibble. The *judex* or *arbiter* was not a lawyer; he was not paid; he was compelled to act, if duly selected; and he was called in for a single case only. For many centuries, only a senator could be selected as a *judex*, but towards the end of the Republic the class of *judices* was enlarged; and in the time of Pliny the register of *judices* numbered several thousands. The patrician institution of the *judices* was balanced by the *Centum-* *Centumviri*, who might be plebeians. These were *viri.* elected, according to Festus, five from each of the 35 tribes, making in all 105. The centumviral tribunal was closely identified with the old institutions of Rome, and asserted a special care of the *jus Quiritium.* Both *judices* and *centumviri* were for Roman citizens. When aliens were admitted to the protection of the civil law, the *judex* or *centumviri* could not be compelled to act; but the spirit of the Roman institution was observed, and the cause was referred to three or five persons *Recupera-* (*recuperatores*) selected by the parties, either one or *tores.* two by each party, with an umpire.

When an action is referred to arbitration, two stages are to be noticed. There is first the reference or selection of the arbitrator, and determination of the question to be referred to him; and secondly, the arbitration itself or the hearing. These two stages are distinguished in Roman Law by terms that have become classical in legal literature, *jus Jus.* and *judicium.* The selection of the arbitrator and *Judicium.* the settlement of the question to be decided took place under the authority of the Prætor (*in jure*); the hearing (*in judicio*) was before the *judex, arbiter, centumviri* or *recuperatores.* The procedure *in judicio* does not call for any remark in this connection; but the procedure *in jure* will repay some consideration.

The mode of reference was at first ORAL, after- Oral wards *in writing.* The written reference was called *Reference.* a *formula;* the oral reference had no distinctive name, but it followed the form of one or other of

Legis
Actiones. the so-called *legis actiones*. The *legis actiones* could not be used by aliens (hence the introduction of *formulae* marks the admission of aliens to civil rights); and, like all the ancient formal proceedings of the Roman Law, could not be employed by an agent or representative of the parties. Every step in the *legis actio* must be taken by the parties themselves.

Sacra-
mentum. The oldest of these forms of process (*sacramentum*) alone calls for notice. It was based on a mock combat, with a pretended voluntary reference to arbitration, and the wager of a sum that was to go to the arbitrator for his trouble. The moveable in dispute, say a slave, was brought before the Praetor. The claimant held a rod (in the place of a spear), and grasping the slave, said, 'This slave I say is mine *ex jure Quiritium*, in accordance with the fitting ground therefor, as I have stated; and so upon thee I have laid this wand,' and at the same time laid the rod on the slave. The opposing party repeated the same words and the same acts. Then the Praetor said, 'Both let go the slave;' they let him go. The first claimant then said, 'I demand that you tell me on what ground you have claimed him;' and he answered, 'I fully told my right as I laid on the wand.' The first claimant retorted, 'Since you have claimed him wrongfully, I challenge you to

wager 500 *asses'* (the *as* was a small coin) ; and
the opposing party, 'In like manner I challenge
thee.' After this ceremony the Praetor inquired
into the merits of the case, and adjudicated the
interim possession to one of the parties ; the other
party then appeared as plaintiff before the *judex,*
to whom the question was referred in this singular
form—not which of the parties was the owner, but
which of them was right in his wager. In this
short drama, which formed the prelude for many
years to every Roman action, we cannot fail to
perceive the true origin of civil jurisdiction—the
submission of disputants to the award of an arbitrator to prevent the effusion of blood.

   The system of *legis actiones* was superseded by *Formulae.*
the use of *formulae.* When the Praetors first determined to administer justice in cases where one of
the parties was alien, they dispensed with the ceremonies exclusively appertaining to the old customs
of Rome, proceeded at once to inquire into the
nature of the dispute, and put in writing the questions to be decided by the arbitrator. The great
superiority of this method recommended it in
quarrels between citizens, to whom the rigorous
and narrow pedantry of the *legis actio* became
odious. By the *lex Aebutia* (B.C. 164 or 170), and
the *leges Juliae* (*temp.* Julius Cæsar or Augustus),
the use of *formulae* was extended to actions be-

tween citizens. The earliest *formulæ* were so framed as to avoid the allegation of an *obligatio.* There would have been a difficulty in saying that an alien had a strict right. Accordingly, the *formula* contained merely allegations of fact, stated hypothetically, followed by an authority to the arbitrator to award damages if the facts were proved. Thus, in the case of deposit, the *formula in factum* ran :—'*Let Lucius Titius be* judex. *If it appears that A. A. deposited with N. N. a silver table, and that, by the fraud of N. N., it has not been given back to A. A., whatever turns out to be the value of the article, that sum of money,* judex, *condemn N. N. to pay A. A. If it does not so appear, acquit him.*' In the case of citizens, there was no reason to shrink from alleging a duty. Accordingly, the *formula in jus* was framed upon a positive allegation of fact, followed by an allegation of legal duty. The allegation of fact was called *demonstratio;* the allegation of legal duty was called *intentio ;* and the power to award damages *condemnatio.* When, as in actions for division of property, an authority was given to assign different parts to the various claimants, the place of the *condemnatio* was taken by the *adjudicatio.* Such a *formula* ran thus :—'*Let Lucius Titius be* judex. *Whereas A. A. sold a slave to N. N. If it appears that N. N. ought to give A. A.* 10,000 sestertii, *then* judex,

Formula in Factum Concepta.

Demonstratio.

Intentio.

Condemnatio.

Adjudicatio.

Formula in jus Concepta.

condemn N. N. to pay 10,000 sestertii *to A. A.
If it does not so appear, acquit him.'* Some-
times another part, called the *exceptio* was intro- *Exceptio.*
duced. In formal contracts or formal transactions
generally, the Roman Law did not originally
allow the defence of fraud; and although the
plaintiff had induced the defendant to bind himself by the grossest fraud, that was not a question into which the *judex* could enter. But, at
length, *Gallus Aquilius*, a colleague of Cicero,
introduced such a defence, and, accordingly, after
his time, the *formula* might embrace a proviso,
'If in that matter nothing has been done, or is
being done, by fraud on the part of the plaintiff.'
Many similar provisions were allowed. ⌊As the *Replicatio.*
exceptio was based on equity, any countervailing
facts could be brought forward in reply by the
plaintiff. This answer to the *exceptio* was called
replicatio.⌋

It thus appears that, viewed as a system of *Defects of*
pleading, the formulary system was rude and *Formulae.*
imperfect. It conveyed the slightest possible
information to the defendant, and scarcely took
more than the first step in eliminating the real
issues between the parties. This—the true end of
all pleading—was thus most inadequately accomplished during the golden era of Roman Jurisprudence.

Interdicts.   In the larger work on Roman Law (p. 836, *sq.*), the nature of interdicts as distinguished from actions is discussed at length ; here it must suffice to say that the interdict was a form of process created by the Practor, and resting upon his authority as a magistrate ; that it was employed mainly to protect rights in the nature of property introduced in his edict ; and that the proceedings were modelled on the ordinary forms of *actio.* In the time of Justinian no formal interdict was granted, and there was nothing to distinguish *interdictum* from *actio* as forms of civil process.

Diocletian's Changes.   The distinction so prominent in Roman Law between *jus* and *judicium* continued until A.D. 294, when Diocletian abolished *judicia*, and enacted that all causes should be heard by judicial officers. The *formula* was no longer used, and its place was occupied by a preliminary discussion to elicit the points in dispute. Hence came the characteristic of the later Roman procedure, that the process which we may not inaptly call pleading, took place before the court itself. Causes were now heard by trained lawyers, instead of private arbitrators, and at last it may be said, the Romans obtained a true civil court.

Execution against the Person.   EXECUTION OF JUDGMENTS.—The natural way of compelling payment of a judgment debt, as it would seem to us, is to take a portion of the debtor's property, if he has any, and sell it to satisfy the judgment creditor. If the debtor has no goods, then we may think of his person and imprison him. This mode of thought shows how far we have advanced from the ideas of the men who built up the fabric of civil jurisdiction. That which we think of as first, was last, and what we regard as last, was first. Execution directly against the property of a judgment debtor was not introduced in Rome until the time of the Emperor Antoninus Pius. The ancient mode of compelling the payment of debts is described to us by Aulus Gellius. The XII Tables provided Law of XII that a debtor was to have thirty days after the Tables judgment debt was proved in order to pay. After that the creditor might arrest him and take him before the Praetor; if the debtor did not find a substitute (*vindex*) to answer for the debt, he was removed by the creditor and put in chains. On three successive market days the creditor was required to bring the debtor before the Praetor and proclaim the amount of his debt. If at the end of sixty days the debt was not paid, the debtor was reduced to slavery. In these proceedings, it is worthy of remark, the initiative is taken, not by the State, but by the creditor. The law interfered only to take precautions in the interest of the debtor, so that no man might unlawfully seize another on the pretext of a debt. These proceedings were essentially a private act of force legalised and subjected to legal restraints. Just as the summons, in its first shape, was purely a private act, in which the law simply made the exercise of force lawful, so in the execution of judgments, the law went no further than a refusal to shield a debtor from his creditor.

Appeals during Republic. APPEALS.—During the Republic, no appeal, properly so called, in a civil cause, existed. But a partial substitute for appeals was found in the right enjoyed by each of the higher magistrates of putting a veto on the acts of any other magistrate. Such a veto was called *intercessio.* The effect of the veto was purely negative ; it stopped for the time the act forbidden, but it could substitute nothing in its place. The concentration of Appeals under Empire. all magisterial power in the hands of the Emperor soon led to the subordination of the tribunals, and the establishment of a final court of appeal. The Emperor was the highest judge, and sometimes heard causes himself; but the *consistorium* or *auditorium*, consisting of the higher officials attached to the Emperor, formed the usual tribunal of ultimate appeal.

APPENDIX.

APPENDIX.

CHAPTER I.

1. What place does Roman Law occupy in General Juris-prudence?

2. Distinguish *jus civile* from *jus gentium*, and explain how the latter came to be identified with the Law of Nature.

3. Explain *leges regiae, jus Papirianum, jus Flavianum,* and *jus Aelianum.*

4. By what agencies is the adaptation of law to the wants of a progressive community accomplished? Compare on this point the history of Roman and English Law.

5. Give an account of the *Jurisprudentes.* In what manner did their labours contribute to the growth of Roman Law? Explain what is meant by the 'law of citation.'

6. Give a brief history of the *Edictum perpetuum.*

7. Upon what principles, and with what leading results, did the Praetor modify and enlarge the *jus civile?*

8. Explain *lex, plebiscitum, populiscitum, senatus con-sultum, constitutio, decretum, epistola, rescriptum.*

9. Give a brief statement of the modes of legislation under the Republic.

10. What attempts at codification were made prior to the time of Justinian?

11. Give an account of the legal achievements in the reign of Justinian. What is Blume's discovery?

12. What is the relation of the Institutes of Justinian to the Institutes of Gaius?

CHAPTER II.

Section I.

13. What place does slavery occupy among the institutions of ancient society?

14. What powers could a master legally exercise over his slave? Is the answer the same for the Republic and the age of the Antonines?

15. In what sense, and to what extent, could a slave enjoy rights of property?

16. In what ways did a person become a slave?

17. Explain *postliminium* and *capitis deminutio.*

18. In what ways could formal manumission be made? Distinguish between the effects of formal and non-formal manumission.

19. Give an account of *Latini Juniani* and *Dedititii.*

20. What restraints on manumission existed in the time of Justinian?

21. What rights had a patron over his manumitted slave?

Section II.

22. What legal powers could a father exercise over his legitimate children?

23. To what extent could a son or daughter under *potestas* enjoy rights of property?

24. Explain the constitution of the Roman family as based on the *patria potestas.*

25. What was *legitimatio per subsequens matrimonium?* In what cases did it apply?

26. What is the true place of adoption in the history of law? What change did Justinian introduce?

27. What was the legal relation of a father to an emancipated son, and to a son who had never been in his *potestas?*

28. Explain the phrases *alieni juris* and *sui juris.*

Section III.

29. Compare the legal position of a slave, a child under *potestas,* and a wife *in manu.*

30. In what way did *manus* become obsolete?

31. What legal relation existed between a husband and a wife not *in manu* ?

32. In what way, and under what restrictions, was divorce sanctioned in the Roman Law ? What provisions were made for the custody of children of divorced parents ?

33. Give an account of the *dos* and *donatio propter nuptias.* Compare the Roman rules with the ordinary provisions of an English marriage settlement.

SECTION IV.

34. Compare the office of *tutor* with the functions of an English trustee or guardian.

35. Explain the phrase *interponere auctoritatem.*

36. Explain the rule of the civil law—*in rem suam auctorem tutorem fieri non posse.*

37. To what extent could a person under puberty acquire legal rights or subject himself to legal duties ?

38. By what modes could a tutor be appointed ?

39. In what cases was security required from *tutores ?*

40. Could a person above the age of puberty obtain relief from an improvident bargain ? What was the advantage of giving a curator to a person above the age of puberty ?

41. To what other persons could curators be appointed ?

CHAPTER III.

SECTION I.

42. Is individual ownership the earliest historical form of property ?

43. Specify the two leading defects of the ancient Roman law of property.

44. What were *res mancipi ?* Describe *mancipatio.*

45. Explain the origin and fate of the distinction between Quiritarian and Bonitarian ownership.

46. By whom, and in what way, was the enjoyment of property in Rome secured to aliens ?

47. *Traditionibus et usucapionibus dominia rerum non nudis pactis transferuntur.* Explain this rule. To what

causes do you attribute its appearance in Roman Law? Illustrate your answer by reference to the rule of English Law.

48. In what various ways could *traditio* be effected?

49. What conditions were necessary to acquire the ownership of a thing by prescription?

50. Distinguish between Positive and Negative Prescription? What was the practical importance of the distinction?

51. What things were *res nullius*, and how could the ownership of them be acquired?

52. What were the several kinds of accession? What is the logical basis of accession, and by what equitable principles was its application accompanied?

53. Upon what principle was the ownership settled of an island formed in a river (1) by accretion in mid-stream, and (2) by a change in the course of the river?

54. Did the Roman Law recognise the right of a tenant farmer to compensation for unexhausted improvements?

55. What was he Roman rule in regard to tenants' fixtures?

56. Did the doctrine of principal and accessory apply in the case of books and pictures?

57. Give an account of *specificatio*, and distinguish from *commixtio* and *confusio*.

58. Explain *res extra nostrum patrimonium* and *res divini juris*.

59. Distinguish and compare *res communes*, *res publicae*, and *res universitatis*.

60. What rights did the public enjoy under the Roman Law in (1) the sea; (2) the sea-shore; (3) rivers; and (4) the banks of rivers?

Section II.

61. Is an estate for life properly described as limited ownership or as a personal servitude?

62. State and criticise the distinction made by the Roman jurists between personal and praedial servitudes.

63. Compare and criticise the distinction made between corporeal and incorporeal things in the English and in the Roman Law respectively.

64. Distinguish usufruct from quasi-usufruct.

65. Compare the rights of a usufructuary of land with the powers of an English tenant for life.

66. What restrictions were imposed on the usufructuary of a house?

67. How was usufruct created and extinguished?

68. Explain *usus, habitatio, operae servorum,* and *precarium.*

Section III.

69. Define 'praedial servitude,' and explain *praedium dominans* and *praedium serviens.*

70. Explain the maxim—*nulli res sua servit.*

71. Distinguish between negative and affirmative servitudes.

72. What is meant by saying that servitudes must be 'perpetual,' that they are 'indivisible,' and that there cannot be a servitude of a servitude?

73. Distinguish urban and rural servitudes. Give the principal examples of each.

74. How were servitudes created and extinguished?

Section IV.

75. What is *emphyteusis?* What controversy as to its juridical place existed, and how was it removed?

76. Give an account of the rights of an *emphyteuta,* and of his superior landlord.

Section V.

77. What was the earliest form of mortgage in the Roman Law, and what were its defects?

78. Distinguish between *pignus* and *hypotheca.* How were they introduced, and in what way did they improve the Roman law of mortgage?

79. How was the 'power of sale' exercised by the mortgagee?

80. Did the Roman Law recognise 'foreclosure?'

81. By what rules was the right of priority determined when the same thing was mortgaged to more than one person?

82. In what cases was a mortgage implied without special agreement?

CHAPTER IV.

SECTION I.

83. Explain the distinction between rights *in rem* and rights *in personam.*

84. To which class of rights does 'contract' belong?

85. What causes led the Roman jurists to take the standpoint of '*obligatio*' instead of its equivalent, 'right *in personam?*'

86. Distinguish 'express contract,' 'implied contract,' and 'quasi-contract.'

87. Is it correct to class delicts with contracts as the two leading groups of '*obligationes?*'

88. Analyse an 'agreement.'

89. Explain *obligatio, conventio, contractus, pactum, pollicitatio, civilis obligatio, honoraria obligatio, naturalis obligatio.*

90. What is meant by essential error, and what are its kinds?

91. What is error *in materia* or *substantia?* State in what cases, according to Savigny, such error vitiated contracts?

92. When can an action be brought for breach of contract, (1) when no time, and (2) when a time has been agreed upon for performance?

93. Could a debtor be sued for breach of contract in a place different from that in which he had agreed to perform his promise?

94. If no place were designated in the contract for performance, where ought an action for breach of contract to be brought?

95. Define 'condition.' Could the condition relate to a past or present event?

96. Distinguish between *dies cedit* and *dies venit.* Apply

the distinction to (1) a conditional contract; (2) an unconditional contract to be performed at a future day; and (3) an unconditional contract to be performed at once.

97. What different rules as to conditions were applied in the law of contract and in the law of wills?

98. Define *vis*, *metus*, and *dolus*. In what cases was a contract invalidated if it was made by one of the parties through *vis*, *metus*, or *dolus?*

99. Give illustrations from the Roman Law of sale of the effects of *suppressio veri* and *suggestio falsi.*

100. If a written security is given against an intended loan, but the money is never lent, can an action be maintained on the security?

101. Explain the maxim—*Impossibilium nulla obligatio est.*

102. What was the *pactum de quota litis?*

103. Show to what extent slaves and *filiifamilias* could bind themselves or their *peculium* by contract.

104. Explain the tardy recognition of agency in the Roman Law.

105. What is necessary to constitute true agency?

106. How far under the later law could slaves and *filiifamilias* act as agents?

107. To what extent was a ship captain an agent for the owner?

108. To what extent was a shopkeeper (*institor*) an agent for his employer?

109. To what extent, according to Savigny, could one free person be agent for another in the later law?

SECTION II.

110. Arrange the contracts of the Roman Law as set forth in the Institutes of Justinian.

111. What are the principles upon which the Roman contracts may be arranged? Compare with the English law.

112. Explain and exemplify *pacta praetoria* and *pacta legitima.*

113. Explain the maxim—*Nuda pactio obligationem non parit, sed parit exceptionem.*

114. Enumerate the characteristics of *naturalis obligatio.*

SECTION III.

115. What is *'nexum ?'*

116. What constituted a *'stipulatio,'* and what were the advantages of recording a stipulation in writing?

117. Explain *cautio, expensilatio, nomen transcriptitium, chirographum, syngrapha.*

SECTION IV.

118. What is *mutuum ?* To what things did it apply?

119. Explain *pecunia trajectitia.*

120. State the purport of the *Senatus consultum Macedonianum.*

121. Define *commodatum.* Under what circumstances was the borrower bound to make good the loss of the thing borrowed?

122. What were the rights of a *commodatarius ?*

123. What is *depositum ?* When was a deposit said to be *miserabile ?* What was the liability of the depositee for misconduct or negligence?

124. Define mandate. Could there be a mandate for the benefit of the *mandatarius* solely? Discuss the question.

125. Enumerate and exemplify the principal cases of mandate.

126. When can a *mandatarius* renounce?

127. Illustrate the proposition that a *mandatarius* must conform to his instructions.

128. What degree of care was incumbent on the *mandatarius ?* Is the mandate an exception to any general rule?

129. What was the relation between a *mandator* and the third parties with whom the *mandatarius* made contracts on his behalf?

130. What rights had a *mandatarius* against a *mandator ?*

131. If a *mandatarius* executed a mandate after the death of the *mandator,* but in ignorance of the fact, was he entitled to the usual rights of a *mandatarius ?*

SECTION V.

132. Define Sale. How was a verbal contract of sale

affected—(1.) By an understanding that it should be committed to writing ; and (2.) By giving earnest ?

133. Could a contract of sale be set aside on the ground of inadequacy or excess in the price ?

134. At what moment was there a contract of sale when the determination of the price was left to a third party ?

135. Explain *vacua possessio.* Why did not the Roman Law require vendors to give the *ownership* of the thing sold ?

136. State in the language of jurisprudence the nature of the right acquired by a buyer in the thing sold in virtue of the contract of sale.

137. At what moment did the interest of a buyer in the thing sold commence ?

138. In what cases did goods sold remain at the risk of the vendor ?

139. State the effect, if buyer or seller were *in mora.*

140. Enumerate the duties of vendor and buyer respectively.

141. Explain the maxim ' *caveat emptor,*' and account for the difference between the Roman and English Law.

SECTION VI.

142. Define *Locatio-conductio.* Distinguish it from *commodatum,* mandate, sale, and the similar innominate contract. Give examples.

143. What was the nature of the right that a tenant of land or houses had in the Roman Law ?

144. What were the duties of a landlord ?

145. Specify the duties of a tenant.

146. Explain the confusion between *locatio operarum* and *locatio operis.*

147. What were the duties of a workman ?

148. State the provisions of the *lex Rhodia de jactu.*

SECTION VII.

149. Define partnership. What is *leonina societas ?*

150. State the broad distinction between the Roman Law of partnership and modern law.

151. By what rules were the shares of partners determined?

152. In what way was partnership ended?

153. Enumerate and distinguish the several kinds of partnership.

154. What were the rights and duties of partners?

SECTION VIII.

155. Enumerate the ways whereby an obligation could be extinguished.

156. In what cases was impossibility an excuse for non-performance of an obligation?

157. Explain and illustrate the statement—*Nihil tam naturale est quam eo genere quidque dissolvere quo colligatum est.*

158. What was the Aquilian Stipulation?

159. Distinguish between the effects of a formal release and a *pactum de non petendo*.

160. When were actions extinguished by lapse of time?

161. Specify and distinguish the three cases to which the name of *novatio* was applied.

162. Was a right *in personam* transferable, and, if so, subject to what conditions?

163. What is *delegatio?* How was it effected? What was the legal presumption established by Justinian in regard to novation?

SECTION IX.

164. In what different ways could suretyship be created? Distinguish them, and arrange them according to their relative antiquity.

165. State the effect of the *Senatus consultum Velleianum.*

166. Could the surety be sued before the principal debtor?

167. In what cases did the discharge of the principal debtor release the surety, and in what cases did the discharge of the surety release the principal debtor? (*See* p. 128.)

168. Had a surety who paid the debt any right of contri-

bution against his co-sureties? State the provisions of the Roman Law on the subject.

Section X.

169. In what cases could money paid by mistake be recovered?

170. Examine the maxim, that ignorance of fact is an excuse, but not ignorance of law.

171. Compare *negotiorum gestio* with mandate.

Section XI.

172. Distinguish *injuria* from *damnum injuria*. Apply your distinction to the case of a slave.

173. Give instances of *injuria*.

174. To what extent was the plea of self-defence available?

175. When was an *injuria* said to be *atrox?*

176. Who had the right of action for an *injuria* done to a person under *potestas* or to a wife?

177. Classify wrongs to property.

178. Define theft. What is meant by stealing the use or possession of a thing?

179. By what principle was it settled when a non-owner could bring an action for theft? Apply the principle to *locatio-conductio, commodatum,* and deposit.

180. What penalties (civil or criminal) were provided by the Roman Law for theft?

181. What was the penalty for robbery?

182. What was the penalty imposed when a person forcibly seized a thing under a *bona fide* claim of right?

183. What were the provisions of the *lex Aquilia?*

184. In what cases was a *directa actio* available under the *lex Aquilia,* and in what cases a *utilis actio* and *actio in factum?*

185. Mention the illustrations of negligence given in the Institutes. What is meant by saying that want of skill is equivalent to negligence?

186. Did the Roman Law take account of consequential damages?

187. What remedies were provided for trespass and ejectment?

188. What is meant by quasi-delict?

189. What liability was incurred by a *judex* giving a wrong decision?

190. What was the penalty for placing or hanging things so as to be a danger in thoroughfares?

191. State the liability of the occupier of a house for damage done by throwing things into thoroughfares.

192. What vicarious responsibility was incurred by ship-masters, innkeepers, and livery-stable keepers?

CHAPTER V.

SECTION I.

193. What contrast does Sir H. S. Maine draw between a will and the instrument from which it is historically derived?

194. How is heirship determined in Hindoo law?

195. Explain ' universal succession,' and ' *damnosa hereditas* ?'

196. What was the ancient character of intestate succession?

197. Explain the position of adoption as a link between intestate succession and wills.

198. What relation existed between the heir and the legatee?

199. State the object and provisions of the *lex Falcidia*.

200. In what way did Justinian enable heirs to escape unlimited liability?

201. What constituted the essence of a Roman will?

202. Enumerate the conditions necessary to a valid *testamentum*.

203. Describe the form of will in the time of Justinian, and explain the origin of its characteristic features.

204. What was disherison? How did the rules on the subject originate?

205. Explain *legitima portio*. Who were entitled to it?

206. Explain *institutio heredis, substitutio vulgaris, sub- stitutio pupillaris*, and *substitutio exemplaris*.

207. When was a *testamentum* said to be *injustum, nullius momenti, inofficiosum, irritum, ruptum* or *destitutum*?

208. Explain how the drawbacks of the testament were got rid of by the use of *codicilli.*

209. How did *codicilli* take effect (1) if there was, and (2) if there was not, a testament?

210. Show how the power of testators was enlarged by trusts (*fideicommissa*).

211. Explain the necessity for, and the provisions of, the *Senatus consulta Trebellianum* and *Pegasianum.*

212. What was the nature and use of the *clausula codicillaris*?

SECTION II.

213. Into what periods may the history of intestate succession in Rome be divided?

214. Give the rules of succession as fixed by the XII Tables.

215. What were the principal changes introduced by the Praetor in intestate succession?

216. State the effects of the *Senatus consulta Tertullianum* and *Orphitianum.*

217. Describe the order of succession as fixed in Justinian's novels.

218. Distinguish *heredes necessarii, heredes sui et necessarii,* and *heredes extranei, beneficium abstinendi, aditio hereditatis.*

SECTION III.

219. What is the basis of the law of legacy?

220. Explain the forms of bequest *per vindicationem, per damnationem, sinendi modo,* and *per praeceptionem.*

221. Give an account of Justinian's fusion of legacies and trusts.

222. What is a *donatio mortis causa*?

223. When property bequeathed was subject to a mortgage, was the heir bound to pay off the mortgage?

224. Could a debt be the object of a legacy?

225. What was the nature of the legatee's right when the legacy was (1) specific, and (2) general?

226. Explain and illustrate the maxims *falsa demonstratio non nocet*, and *falsa causa non nocet.*

227. Could a legacy be left with a restraint on alienation?

228. What restraints on marriage were illegal?

229. If a testator, after making his will, sold or mortgaged a thing left to a legatee, was the legacy thereby revoked?

CHAPTER VI.

230. Discuss the proposition that jurisdiction springs from arbitration.

231. Give a brief sketch of the history of the Roman Summons.

232. Explain the functions of the *judex, arbiter, centumviri,* and *recuperatores.*

233. Explain the distinction between *jus* and *judicium.*

234. What were the *legis actiones?* What were their disadvantages?

235. Give an account of the *sacramentum.*

236. How was the formulary system introduced?

237. Distinguish *formula in factum concepta,* and *formula in jus concepta,* and give an example of each.

238. Explain *demonstratio, intentio, condemnatio, adjudicatio, exceptio, replicatio.*

239. What defects characterised the formulary system?

240. What were *Interdicta?*

241. Explain the nature of the change introduced by Diocletian.

242. Give a historical sketch of the law of execution of judgments.

243. Who first authorised execution against a debtor's property?

244. Was appeal allowed in civil cases (1) under the Republic, and (2) under the Empire?

SUPPLEMENTARY GLOSSARY.

SUPPLEMENTARY GLOSSARY.

Actio, an action, the right of suing before a judge for what is due to one. (J. 4, 6, pr.) Also, proceedings, or a form of procedure, for the enforcement of such right.

Actio arbitraria, an action in which the formula directed the judge, if he found the plaintiff's claim valid, to make an order (*arbitratu tuo, arbitrio judicis*) that the defendant should make amends to the plaintiff,—for instance, give up the thing, or produce it, etc.,—at the same time fixing the sum that in all the circumstances the defendant ought to pay to the plaintiff in case he should fail to make amends as ordered. (J. 4, 6, 31.)

Actio bonae fidei, an equitable action, the formula in which required the judge to take into account considerations of what was fair and right as between the parties. Cf. *Actio stricti juris*. (J. 4, 6, 28-30.)

Actio directa, an action based immediately on the very text of the law; opposed to *actio utilis*. (See *Utilis actio*.) Similarly, an action arising from an essential part of the execution of a contract, as *actio commodati directa*; opposed to *actio (commodati) contraria*, arising, on the other side, from facts that may or may not emerge in the execution of the contract.

Actio hypothecaria, or *quasi-Serviana*. (See p. 73, and J. 4, 6, 7.)

Actio in personam, a personal action; in which the plaintiff claims that the defendant ought to give or do (or make good) something to or for him. The *intentio* runs: 'Si paret Numerium Negidium Aulo Agerio sestertium *X* milia *dare oportere;*' or, 'Quidquid paret Numerium Negidium Aulo Agerio *dare facere oportere.*' (Gaius, 4, 41.)

Actio in rem, a real action ; in which the plaintiff claims
(in the *intentio* of the *formula*, see p. 182) that, as
against all the world, the thing in dispute is his. The
intentio runs : ' Si paret *hominem* (or *fundum*, or *jus
utendi fruendi*, etc.) *ex jure Quiritium Auli Agerii
esse*.'

Actio (in rem) confessoria, an action to try the right to a
servitude, brought by the owner of the dominant land
against the owner of the servient land. (J. 4, 6, 2.)

Actio (in rem) negativa, an action brought by the owner
of the servient land, who alleges that his adversary
is not entitled to a servitude that he is claiming ; or
that he himself is entitled to his land free from the
servitude claimed by his adversary. (J. 4, 6, 2.)

Actio mixta, a mixed action. (1) An action with a view
both to the recovery of a thing and to the enforcement
of a penalty. (J. 4, 6, 18-19.) (2) An action that is both
real and personal ; or, rather, that is entirely personal,
but in one respect more or less similar to a real action ;
for example, the actions *familiae erciscundae, communi
dividundo*, and *finium regundorum*, which involved the
adjudication of particular things to the parties. (J. 4,
6, 20.) (3) ' Actions are mixed in which either party is
plaintiff.' (*Mixtae sunt actiones in quibus uterque actor
est.* Ulpian, *Dig.* 44, 7, 37, 1.)

Actio noxalis, an action brought against a master for
delicts (*noxiae*) committed by his slave (*noxa*) (J. 4, 8) ;
or for damage (*pauperies*) done from wantonness, heat,
or savage nature, by his tame animals. (J. 4, 9.) The
master could free himself from liability by delivering up
the offending slave or animal to the person aggrieved.

Actio praejudicialis, an action preliminary to proceedings,
with a view to ascertain a fact which it is necessary
to establish before going on with the case ; as, whether
a man is free, or is a freedman, or is the son of his
reputed father. (J. 4, 6, 13.)

Actio quod metus causa was open to a person that had
alienated property or undertaken an obligation under
the constraint of intimidation (*metus*) or violence (*vis*).

Actio stricti juris, an action of strict law, the formula in
which limited the attention of the judge to the purely
legal considerations involved. Ct. *Actio bonae fidei*.

Actio utilis. See *Utilis actio.*

Adfinitas, affinity ; the relationship established by marriage between the husband and the kindred of his wife, and between the wife and the kindred of her husband. (J. 1, 10, 6.)

Adjunctio, a form of accession ; the joining of materials belonging to one person with something belonging to another,—*e.g.,* when one weaves another's purple into his own vestment. (J. 2, 1, 26.)

Adolescens, a person between the ages of puberty (14 in boys, 12 in girls) and majority (25).

Adoptio (pp. 29-30). Adoption is the transfer of a person from the *potestas* of one man to that of another. It takes place in two ways. (J. 1, 11, 1.) (1) By imperial rescript ; under authority of which a man may adopt men or women *sui juris.* This mode is called *arrogation.* (See *adrogatio.*) (2) By the authority of a magistrate ; under which a man may adopt men or women *alieni juris.* (Justinian abolished the ancient form of fictitious sales and manumissions, and substituted a mere declaration, recorded in writing before a magistrate. A.D. 530.)

Adrogatio (arrogation), the oldest form of adoption, applicable only in adoption of persons *sui juris.* Originally, it took place under the sanction of the Pontifex, and in the *comitia curiata,* as an act of legislation. Under the Empire, the imperial rescript superseded the legislative proceedings. See *Adoptio,* and p. 30.

Women, not being admitted to the *comitia curiata,* could not be arrogated till the mode by imperial rescript came into use.

Children under puberty were first allowed to be arrogated by Antoninus Pius. In this case, besides the usual inquiries, special investigation was made to render it clear whether the proposed arrogation was for the benefit of the *impubes.* (J. 1, 11, 3.)

Agnati (J. 1, 15, 1 ; 3, 2, 1) are kinsmen related through males—kinsmen, as it were, on the father's side. For a better definition, see p. 167. Agnation is the artificial tie through the *potestas;* cognation, the natural tie through birth. Agnates as tutors (p. 40).

Alieni juris. A person under any one's *potestas, manus* or *mancipium* was said to be *alieni juris,* or *alieno juri subjectus.* (J. 1, 8, pr.)

Alluvio, an imperceptibly gradual deposit of land from a
river (*incrementum latens; per alluvionem id videtur
adjici quod ita paulatim adjicitur ut intelligere non
possis quantum quoquo momento temporis adjiciatur*).
(J. 2, 1, 20.)

Aquae et ignis interdictio, the forbidding one the use of fire
and water.   An indirect mode of depriving one of
citizenship, which could not be done directly.   Cicero
says, '*Civitatem nemo unquam ullo populi jussu amittit
invitus.*'

Auctoritas (from *augeo,* I increase), the 'authority' or
authorisation of a tutor ; the legal capacity in virtue of
which the tutor completed, or filled up what was wanting in, the legal capacity of his pupil (p. 39).

Aversionem, per, in lots, in the lump, *en bloc* (p. 114).

Beneficium competentiae is the name given by the com-
mentators to the privilege of having the *condemnatio*
limited to the extent of a person's means (*quatenus
facere potest*), so that he should not be reduced to want
(*ne egeat*).   (J. 4, 6, 37-38 ; D. 50, 17, 173, and 42, 1, 19.)

Beneficium inventarii.   See p. 154.

Beneficium separationis, the advantage of having a clear
separation made between the property of testator and of
heir.   (J. 2, 19, 1.)

Bona vacantia, property left by a deceased person who has
no successor.   It generally went to the *fiscus.*

Bonorum emptio (or *venditio*),the purchase (or sale) of an insolvent estate (the universal succession of a debtor) by (or to)
one that offers to satisfy the largest proportion of the
claims of the creditors ; a praetorian mode of execution.
[The process under the *judicia extraordinaria* was
called *bonorum distractio.*]

Bonorum possessio (possession of the property) was the
praetorian situation corresponding to civil law *hereditas ;*
an inheritance to which an universal successor succeeded
in virtue of the intervention of the Praetor.

Bonorum possessor was the praetorian heir ; the universal
successor of a deceased person in virtue of the intervention of the Praetor.

Capitale crimen, an accusation affecting the *caput* of the
accused.

Caput, the chief heads of legal status (p. 31, note).

Causa falsa, an untrue ground, or motive; a cause or title wrongly thought to be just or legal. *Error falsae causae* (J. 2, 6, 11), (possession by) mistake, on some untenable ground; mistaken (possession) arising from a fact wrongly supposed to have legal force.

Causa justa, a true or just cause, means, motive, or ground; a legal title—a fact conclusively proving (*e.g.*, an intention to transfer ownership).

Causa liberalis, an *actio praejudicialis* (J. 4, 6, 13), brought to try whether a man was or was not free. Prior to Justinian, an *assertor libertatis* (claimant for freedom) acted for the person whose freedom was in question; but Justinian gave the action directly to the person claiming his freedom.

Causa lucrativa, a ground that is purely gainful. To acquire a thing *lucrativa causa* is to obtain it without a valuable consideration. (J. 2, 20, 6.)

Cautio judicatum solvi. See *Judicatum solvi stipulatio.*

Cautio juratoria, a guarantee by oath (under Justinian); a promise on oath made by a defendant sued in his own name, that he will remain in the power of the Court up to the end of the suit. (J. 4, 11, 2.)

Cognati, persons connected with each other by blood. Cf. *Agnati.*

Cognitor. See under *Procurator.*

Comitia Calata, special meetings of the *Comitia Curiata*, summoned twice a year, and presided over by the pontiff.

Compensatio, set-off; when the defendant brings up his claims against the plaintiff, in order to have them reckoned in reduction of the plaintiff's demand. (J. 4, 6, 39.)

Concubinatus (concubinage) (p. 29), the permanent cohabitation of one man and one woman; differing from lawful marriage in this, that it failed to give the father *potestas* over the children born to him by the concubine. See *Legitimatio.*

Condictio, the general term for a personal action; an action against a person in which the plaintiff alleges in his statement of claim that so-and-so ought to be given to him, or done for him. (J. 4, 6, 15.)

o

Condictio strictly means 'formal notice,' for the plaintiff originally gave formal notice to his opponent to be present to choose a *judex* on the thirtieth day. But this formal notice had ceased to be given by the time of Gaius.

Consilium (J. 1, 6, 4), a public body that (*inter alia*) considered proposals for manumission under the *Lex Aelia Sentia.* It met on certain days at Rome; and it held regular sessions in the provinces, on the last day of which manumission proposals were examined.

Contracts re, contracts arising from a *res*—that is, from some act or fact, namely, the delivery by one person to another of some property with the intention of imposing duties on the receiver.

Creditor, one possessing a personal right against another; one that can compel the performance of an obligation.

Culpa, fault, default, great negligence. 'Magna neglegentia culpa est' (Paul, *Digest*, 50, 16, 226). 'Culpae nomine, id est, desidiae ac neglegentiae' (J. 3, 14, 3, and 3, 25, 9). Culpa was *levis* (slight) or *lata* (gross).
   Culpa levis is incurred when a person falls short either of the care of a *bonus paterfamilias* (*culpa levis in abstracto*), or of the care that he ordinarily gives to his own affairs (*culpa levis in concreto*).
   Culpa lata is incurred by extreme negligence, negligence so gross that it cannot but seem intentional (*dolus*). 'Lata culpa est nimia neglegentia, id est, non intellegere quod omnes intellegunt' (Ulpian, *Digest,* 50, 16, 213, 2). 'Latae culpae finis est non intellegere id quod omnes intellegunt' (Paul, *Digest,* 50, 16, 223, pr.). 'Magna culpa dolus est' (Paul, *Digest,* 50, 16, 226.)

Cum liber erit (J. 1, 14, 1). The appointment of another man's slave as tutor is void, unless made with the condition 'when he becomes free.' (But Ulpian says that such a conditional clause, even if not inserted, is to be implied.)

Cura, curatio, the office or function of the curator.

Curator (p. 41), a guardian appointed to a person past the age of puberty to manage his affairs, when from any cause he is unfit to manage them himself.

Curator bonorum distrahendorum, a curator appointed for the purpose of selling a debtor's property and distributing among the creditors the amount realised.

Debitor, one against whom another possesses a personal right ; one that can be compelled to perform an obligation.

Dedititii, certain manumitted slaves, who, in consequence of grave misconduct committed in the state of slaves, were subjected to certain perpetual disabilities (p. 24).

Defensor, an unauthorised defender, or *procurator voluntarius;* one that without a mandate undertook the defence of another person who had failed to appear in his own defence. (J. 4, 11, 5.)

Defensores, an inferior class of magistrates in provincial towns. (J. 1, 20, 5.)

Deportatio in insulam (p. 31, note), confinement for life within specified bounds ; not necessarily in 'an island.' The person so punished was regarded as civilly dead— a *peregrinus*, no longer a *civis*. He might recover his civil rights, however, by recall and pardon of the emperor. (J. 1, 12, 1.)

Dies fasti, days on which the Praetor could lawfully exercise his general powers.

Dies nefasti, days on which the Praetor could not pronounce any of the words *Do, Dico, Addico;* days on which the court did not sit.

Dies utiles (J. 3, 3, 9), days not *nefasti* after the applicant knew of his right, and was not unavoidably prevented from going on with his case.

Diligentia, diligence, care. There were two grades : (1) *exacta*, all possible diligence ; such care as would be taken by a good or most thoughtful *paterfamilias;* (2) *quantam in suis rebus adhibere solitus est*, the diligence or care a man usually employs in his own affairs.

Divi fratres (J. 1, 25, 6 and 10), the Emperors Marcus Aurelius Antoninus and Lucius Aurelius Verus, who reigned together A.D. 161-169.

Dolus, fraud, wilful injury (p. 86). 'Magna culpa' amounts to *Dolus*. (Paul, *Digest*, 50, 16, 226.)

Dominus litis, the principal in a suit: opposed to his *procurator*.

Donatio, gift. *Donatio inter vivos* (J. 2, 7, 2), when completed, was irrevocable; except in certain cases, especially for ingratitude on the part of the donee. Under Justinian a *donatio* was completed—that is to say, the donor was bound to pass the gift by tradition to the donee—as soon as the donor manifested his intention, whether in writing or not. Before Constantine a mere agreement to give was in no case valid; Constantine made it binding if written.

Donatio propter nuptias, 36 ; *mortis causa,* 172.

Dos, the property contributed by a wife, or by anyone else on her behalf, to her husband, to enable him to support the expenses of the marriage (pp. 35-36).

Duplicatio (doubling), an equitable allegation by a defendant in answer to a *replicatio.*

Emancipatio (pp. 30-31). Three modes : (1) By the ancient process of three fictitious sales, each followed by a manumission ; a mode abolished by Justinian. (2) By imperial rescript, registered by a magistrate; a mode introduced by Anastasius (A.D. 503). (3) The parent went direct before a qualified judge or magistrate, and let his descendant go free from his power; a mode introduced by Justinian. (J. 1, 12, 6.)

Familia (pp. 27, 158), family. It may include (1) all those persons that were subject to the *potestas* of the same individual, whether his children, grandchildren, great-grandchildren, or entirely unconnected with him in blood—free persons or slaves; (2) all descendants of the same ancestors ; (3) all persons connected by agnation ; (4) the slaves of a *paterfamilias;* or (5) the property of a *paterfamilias.* The chief meaning is the first.

Fideicommissarius, the *cestui que trust,* the person to whom, by way of trust, the heir is required to give up the whole inheritance, or a share of it.

Fideicommissum, a trust imposed upon the legal heir for the execution of the last wishes of a deceased person.

Ulpian says, 'A trust is what is left, not by the words of the *jus civile,* but by entreaty ; nor is it from the stiffness of the *jus civile* that it proceeds, but it is given according to the wishes of him that leaves it.'

Fidejussor, a surety ; one that binds himself for the promiser. (J. 3, 20, pr.) A *fidejussor* might be added in every kind of obligation.

Filiusfamilias (son), *filiafamilias* (daughter)—in wider sense, any persons, male or female, under the *patria potestas* of another.

Fundus cum instrumento, a farm with its stock and implements of culture ; including everything on a farm placed there for the purpose of its cultivation and necessary for the cultivation. (J. 2, 20, 17.)

Fundus instructus, a farm with its furnishing ; with everything upon it, useful or ornamental, including not only stock and implements, but also everything prepared for the comfort or pleasure of the owner.

Furtum conceptum is a term applied when in a man's house, before witnesses, something that has been stolen is sought and found. An *actio concepti* lies against the occupier.

Furtum oblatum is a term applied when something that has been stolen is brought to a man by some one, and is found on formal search in his house ; that is, if brought to him with the intention that it should be found in his house and not in the bringer's. The occupier has an *actio oblati* against the bringer.

Hereditas (inheritance) is the succession (in virtue of civil law rights) to the whole legal position of a deceased person (*nihil aliud est quam successio in universum jus quod defunctus habuit*). Cf. *Bonorum possessio*.

Heres (heir), the universal successor of a deceased person, in virtue of his rights under the *jus civile*. He might be appointed by will or take *ab intestato*.

Heres fiduciarius, an heir that has a *fideicommissum* entrusted to him to carry out.

Impubes, a person below the legal age of puberty ; a male under 14, or a female under 12.

Incerta persona, a person that is not a specific living individual ; an indeterminate person. A legatee was held to be indeterminate when the testator added him with an indeterminate notion of him in his mind : as

'the man that comes first to my funeral,' 'whoever
bestows on my son his daughter in marriage.' (J. 2,
20, 25.)

Infans, strictly, a child not yet able to speak. Later, a child
under the age of seven.

Infanti proximus, a child that can indeed speak, but not yet
with understanding (*intellectus*); a child that has not
passed his seventh year.

Ingenuus, a freeborn man, a man free from the moment of
his birth ; being born in wedlock, the son of parents that
either are freeborn or have been made free. (J. 1, 4, pr.)

Inquisitio, inquiry ; made in certain cases by the Praetor (or
Praeses), as preliminary to the confirmation of persons
appointed tutors or curators.

Interdicta, formulae framed and used by the Praetor, by
which he ordered or forbad something to be done,
chiefly in disputes about possession or quasi-possession.
(J. 4, 15, pr.)

Intestatus. 'A man dies intestate if he has not made a will
at all, or if he has made it wrongly, or if the will he had
made has been broken or become null, or if no one is
heir under it.' (J. 3, 1, pr.)

Judicatum solvi stipulatio, a stipulation whereby a plaintiff
took security, at the beginning of a suit, for satisfaction
of the judgment.

 (1) *Before Justinian.*—In a *real* action, commenced
by *formula petitoria* (Gaius, 4, 91), the defendant was
required to give the *cautio judicatum solvi,*—security
with sureties, so that, if judgment went against him, and
he neither restored the thing in dispute, nor paid its
value, the plaintiff might be able to proceed against him
and his sureties (G. 4, 89 ; J. 4, 11, pr.) The stipulation
included three clauses : *de re judicata, de re defendenda,
de dolo malo* (*Dig.* 46, 7, 6). The first guaranteed that
the amount adjudged by the sentence should be paid, in
case the defendant should not restore the thing ; the
second, that the action should be properly defended—
that is, conducted, under further securities, through all
its steps, down to the judgment, and the payment of the
amount adjudged ; and the third, that no malicious
injury should be done to the thing.

In a *personal* action, the defendant, if sued in his own name, did not give security *judicatum solvi*, except in a few special cases. If he appeared by a *cognitor*, he must give security for the *cognitor;* if by a *procurator*, the *procurator* himself gave securities. (G. 4, 101.)

(2) *Under Justinian.*—Justinian did not maintain the distinction between real and personal actions. The defendant, if sued in his own name, was required to give security for the second clause of the stipulation *judicatum solvi*,—namely, that he would appear personally, and remain in court to the end of the trial. (J. 4, 11, 2.) If represented by a procurator, appointed by him personally in court, the defendant bound himself for the procurator for all three clauses ; if represented by a procurator appointed outside the court, he became *fidejussor* for his procurator, and both were bound for all three clauses. In either case, he was required to mortgage the whole of his property as security—an arrangement that bound his heirs ; and, moreover, he must give further security that he would come up to receive the judgment.

Failing the appearance of the defendant,—a voluntary or unauthorised *defensor* was accepted, but he must give security *judicatum solvi*. (J. 4, 11.)

Judicia publica, public prosecutions ; so called, because generally it was open to any citizen to institute them and carry them through.

Jurisprudentia, law-learning, the learning of the *jurisprudentes* (men skilled in the law : see pp. 6-10), 'the knowledge of things divine and human, of the just and the unjust.' (J. 1, 1, 1.)

Jus, in its widest sense, includes moral as well as legal obligations ; Celsus defines it as the art of distinguishing the good and the fair (*ars boni et aequi*).

In its strictly legal application, *jus* (1) generally means 'law,' as opposed to *lex* (a statute) ; (2) a 'right,' as *jus itineris* (right of way) ; (3) more vaguely, 'relationship,'—as *jus cognationis vel adfinitatis* (the *tie* of blood or affinity) ; (4) by metonymy, the 'court' of the magistrate. (See p. 179.)

Jus accrescendi, the right of accrual.

If a slave was owned in common by Titius and

another, and that other alone gave the slave freedom, in that case the liberating owner's share was lost to him and accrued to his partner. (J. 2, 7, 4.)

If one of several persons nominated heir for any reason does not become heir, his share is divided among such as become heirs, in proportion to their respective shares. (J. 3, 4, 4.)

If daughters, or other descendants through males, whether male or female, were neither named as heirs in the will nor disinherited, the will was not thereby avoided ; only these were afforded a right to come in for a certain share along with the heirs appointed in the will. (J. 2, 13, pr.)

Jus aedilicium, the rules of law as stated in the edicts published by the curule aediles, and administered by them. It was included in the *jus honorarium.* (J. 1, 2, 7.)

Jus Civile, (1) the law peculiar to a particular state ; as opposed to the *jus gentium* (the law common to all peoples), and *jus naturale.* Hence, the peculiar local law *of Rome.* (2) The old law of Rome, as opposed to the later *jus praetorium* or *honorarium* (introduced by the Praetor). In this sense, it includes the law peculiar to the city of Rome, and such portions of the *jus gentium* as were recognised by the old law. (J. 1, 2, 1 and 2 ; J. 2, 1, 11. See p. 3.)

Jus Gentium, the law common to all peoples. (J. 1, 2, 1 and 2.) Opposed to *jus naturale* and *jus civile.*

Jus honorarium. See *Jus Praetorium.*

Jus liberorum, the special rights granted to the mother of three or four children (J. 3, 3, 2) ; or to the father (J. 1, 25, pr.). Compare also Gaius, 1, 194.

Jus naturale. 'the law that nature has taught all living things' (J. 1, 2, pr. : after Ulpian) ; the law supposed to be constituted by right reason common to nature and to man. Opposed to *jus gentium* and *jus civile.* Sometimes, however, identified with *jus gentium* (J. 1, 2, 11). See pp. 2, 3.

Jus non scriptum, the unwritten law, 'the law that use has approved." (J. 1, 2, 9.)

Jus potestatis, or *patria potestas* (p. 26).

Jus Praetorium the rules of law as stated in the Praetor's edict, and administered by the Praetor. Also called *jus honorarium*. It included the *jus aedilicium*. (J. 1, 2, 7. See pp. 10, 12.)

Jus Privatum, the department of law that looks to the advantage of individuals ; that deals with causes between private individuals.

It was said to be threefold (*tripertitum*), as being gathered from the precepts of the *jus naturale*, of the *jus gentium*, and of the *jus civile*. (J. 1, 1, 4.) Distinguish other cases of *jus tripertitum* (pp. 7, 157). It is divided into three parts, according as it relates to Persons, Things, or Actions. (J. 1, 3, pr.)

Jus Publicum, the department of law that looks to the standing of the affairs of Rome ; that deals with causes between the State and private individuals. It embraces Ecclesiastical Law, Constitutional Law (including the Administration), and Criminal Law. (J. 1, 1, 4.)

Jus scriptum, the written portion of the law, consisting of statutes, decrees of the *plebs*, decrees of the senate, decisions of emperors, edicts of magistrates, and answers of jurisprudents. (J. 1, 2, 3.)

Jus tripertitum (pp. 7, 157). See also *Jus Privatum* and *Testamentum*.

Justitia, 'the constant and perpetual wish to give each man his due' (*jus suum*). (J. 1, 1, pr.)

Legatarius partiarius, a legatee to whom the testator has in his will instructed his heir to give a definite share of his universal succession (*hereditas*).

This kind of legacy was called a legacy of partition (*legatum partitionis*), because the legatee divided the inheritance with the heir. (J. 2, 23, 5.)

Legatum (legacy), any gift from a deceased person (*donatio quaedam a defuncto relicta*).

Legatum generis, a legacy of a thing in general terms ; a legacy of something that is indicated by the testator only as belonging to a class (*generaliter legatur*) ; as 'a slave.' (J. 2, 20, 22.) But the class must not be too wide, as 'an animal.'

Legatum nominis, a legacy of a debt (*quod defuncto debetur*). (J. 2, 20, 21.)

Legatum optionis, a legacy of choice; where the testator directs the legatee to choose from among his slaves or other property. (J. 2, 20, 23.)

Legatum partitionis. See *Legatarius partiarius*.

Legatum poenae nomine. A legacy was regarded as given by way of penalty when the purpose was to constrain the heir to do or not to do something. (J. 2, 20, 36.)

Legitimatio (legitimation) of the children of concubinage (*naturales liberi*) was effected in three modes. (1) By subsequent marriage of the parents (p. 29), introduced by Constantine (A.D. 335), abrogated by Zeno (A.D. 476), and revived and amplified by Justinian (A.D. 529). (2) By offering the natural child to the curia (*per oblationem curiae*); making a son a *decurio*, or member of the class that furnished the magistrates in provincial towns, or giving a daughter in marriage to a *decurio*. (3) By rescript of the emperor; introduced by Justinian.

Lex Hortensia (B.C. 287) provided that *plebiscita* should bind the whole people equally with *leges*. (J. 1, 2, 4.)

Lex Hostilia extended the cases where one person was permitted to bring an action on account of another. It allowed an action for theft to be brought on account o persons that were among the enemy or away in the service of the commonwealth, or that were in the *tutela* of some person bringing the action. (J. 4, 10, pr.)

Lex Regia, the statute by which the people vested the supreme power in the emperor. (J. 1, 2, 6.)

Libertas, freedom, the capacity to possess the rights and to fulfil the duties of a free person; 'the natural right each man has of doing what he pleases, except in so far as he is hindered by force or by law.' (J. 1, 3, 1.)

Libertas directa, fideicommissaria. The gift of freedom was said to be made directly (*libertas directa*) when a master set free his own slave,—as when he appointed his slave as a tutor; for either the testator accompanied the appointment with express enfranchisement, or the law implied his intention to do so. When the testator appointed as a tutor another man's slave, entrusting it to his heir to purchase and enfranchise the slave, freedom thus given indirectly through a trust was called *libertas fideicommissaria.*

Libertinus, a freedman ; a man that has been set free from lawful slavery by manumission. (J. 1, 5, pr.)
Three classes (before Justinian) : (1) Such as became full Roman citizens ; (2) *Latini Juniani* ; (3) *Dedititii.* See pp. 23, 24. (J. 1, 5, 3.)

Literarum obligatio (or *expensilatio*) was created by an entry in the account books (*codex*) of the creditor, with the consent of the debtor, charging the debtor as owing a certain sum.

Manumissio, the giving a slave his freedom ; the setting a slave free from the 'hand' or *potestas* of his master. (J. 1, 5, pr.)
Formal, public or legal manumission (*manumissio legitima, solemnis,* or *justa*) was effected in one of three modes recognised by the old law : (1) *Vindicta;* (2) *Censu;* (3) *Testamento.* (See pp. 22, 23.) Also, in later times, (4) in Church.
Informal manumission took place (1) by an oral declaration of freedom in presence of friends (*inter amicos*) ; (2) by letter (*per epistolam*) ; or (3) by any other expression of a man's last will. Witnesses were necessary in each case. Other methods were introduced in various imperial constitutions.

Manus, marital power (literally 'hand'). See pp. 22, follg.
Three modes whereby a woman was subjected to the *manus* of her husband : (1) *Confarreatio;* (2) *Coemptio* (fictitious sale) ; (3) *Usus* (cohabitation).

Matrimonium. See *Nuptiae.*

Minor (viginti quinque annis). The age of minority extended from puberty (12 or 14) up to 25 (p. 41).

Naturales liberi, natural children. (1) Children not born in lawful wedlock ; opposed to *legitimi.* (J. 1, 10, 13.) (2) Children born to us : opposed to *adoptivi.* (J. 1, 11, pr.)

Novatio, the renewal or new-making of an existing obligation ; the transmutation of an obligation, so that it ceases to exist and is revived as a new obligation. '*Novatio* est prioris debiti in aliam obligationem vel civilem vel naturalem transfusio atque translatio : hoc est, cum ex

praecedenti causa ita nova constituatur ut prior peri-
matur." (Ulpian, *Dig.* 46, 2, 1.) The preceding
obligation may have been contracted in any form, and
with any subject; the new obligation must be *verbis* (or
literis), and it must bind either civilly or naturally.

Nuptiae (marriage—strictly the ceremonies with which the
legal tie was formed), or *matrimonium* (matrimony,
strictly, the tie itself), is the union of a man and a
woman, involving unbroken harmony in the habits of
life. (J. 1, 9, 1.) Marriage (*justae nuptiae*) may be defined as that particular union of the sexes that gave the
father *potestas* over the children born to him by his
wife. (Cf. J. 1, 10, pr., and 12.) See pp. 32, follg., and
Manus.

   Conditions of *justae nuptiae:* (1) Consent of the
parties duly expressed; (2) Puberty of the parties (man
must be 14, woman 12); (3) *Conubium* (or legal power
of contracting marriage) of the parties,—*i.e.* (*a*) they
must have the rights of citizenship, so far as implied
in *conubium;* (*b*) they must be without the prohibited
degrees of relationship; and (*c*) they must have obtained
the consent of their *patresfamiliarum* (if under *potestas*).

Obligatio civilis, an obligation either established by statute,
   or at all events recognised by the *jus civile.*

Obligatio literarum. See *Literarum obligatio.*

Obligatio praetoria or *honoraria,* an obligation established
   by the Praetor in the exercise of his jurisdiction.

Obligatio verborum. See *Verborum obligatio.*

Oratio, an address by the emperor to the senate, stating
   what he wished them to embody in a *senatus consultum.*
   (J. 2, 17, 7-8.)

Orcinus, pertaining to Orcus (Pluto), the nether world, or
   death. A freedman was so called (*orcinus*) who had
   received freedom directly from the will of his master,
   having been the slave of the testator at the date of the
   will as well as at the time of his death. (J. 2, 24, 2.)

Paterfamilias (pp. 20, 26), anyone invested with *patria
   potestas* over another; or any man *sui juris,* or not
   under the authority of another.

Patria potestas, the rights enjoyed by the head of a Roman family (*paterfamilias*) over his legitimate children. (J. 1, 9, pr. See pp. 26, follg.)

Acquired (1) by birth, (2) by legitimation, (3) by adoption.

Dissolved (1) by death of *paterfamilias*, (2) by parent's or child's suffering loss of *status*, (3) by son's being raised to the patriciate, (4) by emancipation.

Patriciatus, the patriciate (J. 1, 12, 4); from the time of Constantine, the highest rank at court.

Patrimonium. Things *in nostro patrimonio* are things belonging to individuals. Things *extra nostrum patrimonium* (p. 57), are things belonging, not to individuals, but to all men (*communes*), to the state (*publicae*), to corporate bodies (*universitatis*), or to no one (*nullius*).

Pauperies, mischief occasioned by an animal; damage done without *injuria*, or wrong intent, on the part of the doer. (J. 4, 9.) See *Actio.noxalis*.

Persona, (1) a being or entity (person, corporation, etc.) capable of enjoying legal rights; (2) a being (person, corporation, etc.) capable of enjoying legal duties; (3) a man's political and social rights collectively, his legal character or capacity, as *persona patris* (the character or legal relations of father). Also, simply a human being.

Persona extranea, a person outside one's family; that is, not in one's *potestas, manus*, or *mancipium*, nor *bona fide* possessed by one, nor held as a slave in usufruct. *Per extraneam personam nihil adquiri potest;* such an outsider could not acquire anything for one.

Persona incerta. See *Incerta persona.*

Persona publica, a public officer. Applied (J. 1, 11, 13) to a notary.

Placita principum. See *Principum placita.*

Plus-petere, plus or *pluris-petitio*, is when the plaintiff claims more than he is entitled to. This might be done in four ways : *re, tempore, loco, causa.* (J. 4, 6, 33.)

Poena, a penalty, is the punishment of an offence (*noxae vindicta*), generally inflicted for delicts. It is not confined to a money payment, as *multa* (a fine) is, but may extend to the *caput* and *existimatio* of the offender.

It is not left to the discretion of the judge, like *multa*, but is specially appointed for each particular delict by a statute or by some other form of law. (Ulpian, *Dig.* 50, 16, 131.) The Twelve Tables made *furtum manifestum* a capital offence: a freeman was scourged, and adjudged to the man he had stolen from; a slave was scourged and put to death. But this harshness shocked the public sense, and the Praetor fixed the penalty at fourfold the amount. (Gaius, 3, 189, 190. Cf. J. 4, 4, 7.)

Poenae servus. See *Servus poenae.*

Possessio, legal possession, is the detention or physical apprehension of a thing (*detentio*), with the intention of holding it as one's own (*animus possidendi*). *Possessio* was protected by interdicts.

In possessione esse, 'to be in possession of' a thing, not 'to possess it,' the *animus possidendi* being absent.

Possessio civilis, civil possession, was possession capable of ripening into ownership by usucapion. It had three conditions: the thing possessed (1) must be free from *vitium* of any kind (J. 2, 6, 10); (2) must be held *ex justa causa;* and (3) *bona fide.*

Possessio naturalis, natural possession, was where a person either possessed a thing not *ex justa causa* and *bona fide*, or was simply 'in possession of' it. *Possessio naturalis* was not protected by interdicts.

Possidere pro herede, to possess in the belief that one is heir. (J. 4, 15, 3.)

Possidere pro possessore, to possess a part or the whole of an inheritance, without any right, and with the knowledge that it does not belong to one. (J. 4, 15, 3.)

Postumus, (1) a child of a testator, *born after his death*, who, if born in his lifetime, would have been under his *potestas*, and entitled to succeed him if he died intestate; (2) a child of a testator conceived before the date of the will, but born his *suus heres, after the date of the will*, and before the testator's death. This was called a *postumus Vellaeanus*, from *lex Junia Vellaea* (A.D. 27?), which provided that the testator might institute or exclude such a child.

Postumus alienus, a posthumous stranger; a posthumous child that would not have been under the testator's power if born in his lifetime. (J. 2, 20, 28.)

Praedia stipendiaria, provincial lands belonging peculiarly to
the Roman people, and paying taxes (*stipendia*).

Praedia tributaria, provincial lands belonging peculiarly to
the emperor, and paying tribute (*tributum*).

Praefectus urbi, the city prefect or governor. His civil jurisdiction extended to one hundred miles round Rome
and his criminal jurisdiction throughout Italy. He
overshadowed the Praetor, from whom an appeal lay
to him. The office was restored and placed on its new
basis by Augustus.

Praeses, the president or governor of a province, originally of
a senatorian or popular province; a *legatus Caesaris*
being the governor of a province reserved by the
emperor.

Principum placita, the enactments (or constitutions) of the
emperors. 'What the emperor determines has the
force of a statute' (*quod principi placuit legis habet
vigorem*). See p. 14. (J. 1, 2, 6.)

Procinctum. See *Testamentum.*

Procurator, an agent appointed by mandate to act for another in all actions, or only in a single action. He may
be appointed when present, or by messenger, or by
letter, and under any conditions, or any arrangements
as to time; and in the absence or without the knowledge
of the opposite party. No special words are needed.
(*Dig.* 3, 3, 1-4.) 'Some think,' says Gaius (4, 84),
'that a man must be held to be a procurator if only,
though no mandate is given him, he comes to the
business in good faith, and gives security that the principal will ratify what he does.' (J. 4, 10.)

The older agent, *cognitor,* was appointed only for a
single action, by a set form of words, and in the presence of the opposite party. He need not be present at
the ceremony, but he does not become *cognitor* unless
and until he consents and undertakes the office. Gaius
(4, 83) gives the formula of appointment. By the time
of Justinian, the *cognitor* was superseded by the *procurator.*

Proprietas nuda, or *proprietas deducto usufructu,* bare ownership; ownership without usufruct—the ownership of property of which another person has the usufruct.

Prudentium responsa. See pp. 8-10. (J. 1, 2, 8.)

Pubertas, the legal age of puberty ; 14 for males, 12 for females. *Plena pubertas* (J. 1, 11, 4) was fixed at 18, when the body was regarded as fully developed.

Pubertati proximi, children in the stage next to puberty ; that is, from the beginning of. their eighth year until they have passed the age of puberty. According to some, a period of about a year before puberty.

Pupillus, a person *sui juris*, under the age of puberty, whose affairs are managed, and whose want of legal capacity is supplied, by a tutor. (See pp. 37-41.)

Quarta Antonina, or *Quarta D. Pii*. An arrogated son under puberty, if disinherited, or emancipated without lawful cause, received back all the property he had brought to the arrogator or acquired for him, and also *one-fourth* of the arrogator's property. This was enacted by Antoninus Pius. (J. 1, 11, 3.)

Relegatio, banishment, in the sense of prohibition to enter Rome, or one's province, or any particular district, either for life or for a limited term ; it may also be restriction to a particular place. This punishment did not affect one's *status*, or property, or *potestas*. (J. 1, 12, 2.)

Reus, strictly any party to a case. 'Reos appello quorum res est' (Cicero). Applied, in case of an obligation, to stipulator or promiser. 'Qui stipulatur, *reus stipulandi* dicitur ; qui promittit, *reus promittendi* habetur.' (Modestinus, *Dig.* 45, 2, 1.) Then, a person subject to an obligation ; a defendant. (J. 3, 29, pr.) But such a development of the applications is not certain.

Ruptum (broken, smashed), in the *lex Aquilia*, means spoiled (*corruptum*) in any way. 'And therefore not only breaking and burning, but also cutting and crushing and spilling, and in any way destroying or making worse, are included under this term. Nay, an opinion has been given that if a man puts anything into another's wine or oil to spoil its natural goodness, he is liable under this part (the third head) of the statute.' (J. 4, 3, 13.)

A will, valid when made, becomes *ruptum* in two ways : (1) by subsequent agnation of a *suus heres*, and (2) by the making of a new will.

Semestria, half-yearly ordinances, the records of the half-yearly imperial council of senators. (J. 1, 25, 1.)

Servitus, slavery, 'an institution of the *jus gentium*, by which, contrary to nature, a man becomes the property of a master.' (J. 1, 3, 2; cf. 1, 5, pr.)

In servitute esse (J. 1, 4, 1), 'to be in the position of a slave'—not to be actually a slave.

Servus ordinarius, a slave holding some special post in the establishment, as cook, baker, etc. (J. 2, 20, 17.)

Servus poenae, a slave of punishment, a convict. Such were slaves sent to the mines, or condemned to fight with wild beasts. (J. 1, 12, 3.) They were so called because, though slaves, they had no personal master. Justinian abolished the class, and prohibited the infliction of slavery as a punishment for crime.

Servus vicarius, an attendant or assistant of a *servus ordinarius*. (J. 2, 20, 17.) Often purchased by the *ordinarius*, out of his *peculium*, to do part of his work.

Sponsus (betrothed). In Latium (and, indeed, also in Rome) the man that intended to marry a woman stipulated with the person that was to give her in marriage that he would do so, and on his part promised (*spondebat*) to marry her. The woman thus promised was called *sponsa;* the man that promised to marry her was called *sponsus*. *Sponsalia* denoted the proposal and the reciprocal promise of a future marriage.

Spurii (bastards), persons born out of lawful marriage. (J. 1, 10, 12.)

Stipulatio, strictly, the act of a stipulator, the putting of the question to the promiser. Hence, the whole of the formality gone through by both stipulator and promiser. Then, a contract entered into with this formality.

Stipulations were said to be *judiciales* (by order of a *judex*), *praetoriae* (by order of a Praetor), *communes* (by order sometimes of a *judex*, sometimes of the Praetor), or *conventionales* (by agreement of the parties themselves).

Stuprum, any connection between a man and an unmarried free woman (not a slave) otherwise than in concubinage.

Sui juris. A person not subject to any of the three forms of authority, *potestas, manus, mancipium*, was said to be *sui juris* (independent). (J. 1, 8, pr.)

Tabulae. Secundum tabulas testamenti, according to the

P

tablets (or terms) of the will. *Contra tabulas testamenti*, in opposition to the provisions of the will.

Tabularius, a public notary; so called from the *tabulae* (public registers of formal acts) kept by him.

Testamenti factio, capacity to take any part in making a will, or any benefit under a will.

Testamentum destitutum (p. 161), an abandoned will,—when no one entered on the inheritance. This was one of the forms of *testamentum irritum*.

Testamentum militare, a will made by a soldier on actual service, in writing or orally, without any formality. Granted temporarily by Julius Caesar, subsequently renewed by several emperors, and established permanently by Trajan. (J. 2, 11.)

Testamentum procinctum, or *in procinctu factum*, a will made on the eve of battle. *Procinctus est expeditus et armatus exercitus. Procinctus* means an army without baggage and in arms. (G. 2, 101.)

Testamentum tripertitum. The written will of the time of Justinian was spoken of as *jus tripertitum*, as deriving its elements from three sources. The witnesses and their presence together for the single purpose of publishing the will come down from the *jus civile;* the signatures of the testator and of the witnesses, from the imperial constitutions; and the seals of the witnesses and their number (seven), from the Praetor's edict. (J. 2, 10, 3.)

Thesaurus, treasure trove (p. 52), treasure deposited in a place for so long a time that it has been forgotten, and now has no owner (*vetus quaedam depositio pecuniae cujus non extat memoria, ut jam dominum non habeat*). (D. 41, 1, 31, 1.)

Triplicatio (tripling), an equitable allegation by a plaintiff in answer to a *duplicatio*.

Tutela, tutelage, tutory, guardianship ; the public and unpaid duty imposed by the civil law on one or more persons of managing the affairs and removing the legal incapacities of a person *sui juris*, under the age of puberty. The definition of Servius (J. 1, 13, 1) is defective, in omitting to state (1) that *tutela* was a public office or duty, which the person duly appointed could not refuse to undertake ; and (2) that it was an unpaid office.

Tutor, a person on whom the civil law has imposed the public and unpaid duty of managing the affairs and removing the legal incapacities of a person *sui juris* under the age of puberty. (See pp. 37-41.)

Tutor Atilianus, or *Juliotitianus*, a tutor given to a pupil that had no tutor at all,—in Rome, by the urban Praetor and a majority of the (ten) tribunes of the commons, under the *lex Atilia* (before B.C. 197); in the provinces, by the presidents of the provinces, under the *lex Julia et Titia* (about B.C. 31).

Tutor dativus, tutor appointed by an authorised magistrate (p. 40).

Tutor fiduciarius, a tutor holding office as if on a trust committed to him by the father. If a *paterfamilias* emancipated a descendant, and then died, leaving male descendants alive, such male descendants became the fiduciary tutors of their emancipated brother or sister, or sons, and so forth. (J. 1, 19, pr.)

Tutor honorarius. In cases where the administration of a pupil's property was confided to some of the tutors, to the exclusion of others, the tutors so excluded were called *tutores honorarii.* (J. 1, 24, 1.)

Tutor legitimus, a statutory tutor, a tutor that succeeded to the office under the provisions of some statute, and particularly of the XII Tables (p. 40). Such, in the first instance, were the pupil's *agnati.*

Tutor onerarius was one that bore the burden of acting (as opposed to *tutor honorarius*). (J. 1, 24, 1.)

Tutor testamentarius, a tutor appointed by the' last will, or by *codicilli* confirmed by the last will, of the deceased *paterfamilias* of the *pupillus* (p. 40). (Both Gaius and Ulpian call such tutors *dativi.* Better, with Justinian, to confine *dativi* to tutors appointed by magistrates.)

Universitas. (1) A corporate body. *Res universitatis*, corporate property; opposed to *res singulorum*, individual property (p. 58).

(2.) The totality or aggregate of rights and duties inhering in any individual man, and passing to another as a whole at once (*universitas juris*). The chief example is Inheritance. Opposed to *res singulae*, particular things or aggregates of things.

Utilis actio, an action granted by the Praetor, in the exercise of his judicial authority, by means of an extension of an existing action, to persons or cases that did not come within its original scope. The existing action, on which the *actio utilis* was based, was called by contrast *actio directa.*

Utilis annus, a year of *dies utiles*, made up by reckoning in succession only the days on which the plaintiff could bring his action (*experiundi potestatem habuit*); that is, the days on which the Praetor sat, and on which neither plaintiff nor defendant was unavoidably hindered from being present in person or being represented by a procurator. (Ulpian, *Dig.* 44, 3, 1.)

Verborum obligatio, a verbal obligation, is contracted by means of a question and an answer, when we stipulate that anything shall be given to us or done for us. It is the *stipulatio.* (J. 3, 15, pr.)

Vindicatio, the general word for a real action. (J. 4, 6, 15.) Also, specially, the usual real action by which a title to any real property could be made out. It was brought by the owner (*dominus*) alone, against the person in possession of the property in dispute. The burden of proof rested on the claimant (*petitor*); the defendant was not bound to show that he had any title whatever.

Vocatio in jus, summons before the magistrate.

INDEX.

INDEX.

EDINBURGH
COLSTON AND COMPANY
PRINTERS

47464.

www.ingramcontent.com/pod-product-compliance
Lightning Source LLC
Chambersburg PA
CBHW030816020726
47499CB00006B/1940